Translucent Tree

NOBUKO TAKAGI

TRANSLATED BY
DEBORAH IWABUCHI

VERTICAL.

Translucent Tree

VERTICAL.

Translucent Tree

I

THE TOWN OF TSURUGI is located at the point where the Tedorigawa River, which flows out of Mt. Hakusan and runs through the Kaga Plain into the Japan Sea, releases itself from the mountain's confines and widens its arms under the bright light of day. Kaga Ichinomiya Station, a stop on the Ishikawa Line, is located in the town's center. A further thirty-minute ride north through the rice fields on the single-track line will take you to Nomachi Station near Saikawa River. Nowadays you can get there by car in twenty minutes, and the area is growing as houses go up and people have begun commuting into the city of Kanazawa. In the old days, Tsurugi was a prosperous town on its own where pilgrims began their approach to Hakusan, an object of worship.

The name, Tsurugi, written with the characters for "crane" and "come," evokes the sound of wings against the wind and the arrival of flocks of the great birds. It makes sense considering all the myths and legends surrounding the area, but the name originally had to do with swords—also *tsurugi* in Japanese. The town originally grew up outside the compound of Kingengu, or Golden Sword Shrine, and was known for the *katana*, single-edged Japanese swords, it forged.

About six hundred and fifty years ago, during the time the Togashi clan ruled the Kaga Plain, there was a swordsmith named Tomoshige Fujishima who moved to the area from Echizen. His family had fled to the mountains of Etchu to avoid the Ikko uprising of Buddhist zealots and returned to the flatlands, to Matsuto in the northern part of Tsurugi, when Toshiie Maeda succeeded in suppressing the rebellion.

In a more peaceful era, most of the swordsmiths in the area were reduced to making plows, hoes, and other farming tools. Still, for hundreds of years, even after there was no longer work even for common blacksmiths and swords were produced only as works of art, a very few families in the area quietly passed the craft of swordmaking from one generation to the next.

The last of these craftsmen was Kaho Yamazaki, who died in 1983, in poverty and following a long illness, at the age of eighty-six. Not long after he turned sixty, he began to suffer from the pain in the back and shoulders characteristic of blacksmiths, but the cause of his death was lung cancer. No one could be sure whether it was from all the years of inhaling iron shavings and the flames of his furnace or the fifty cigarettes he smoked each day.

At any rate, eighty-six years amounted to a long life, and the death of Kaho meant the end of the long history of swordmaking in Tsurugi.

As for the surname of Yamazaki, Kaho believed until the day he died that when Fujishima the swordmaker escaped to Etchu, he was given shelter there by the family of Kanzaburo Yamazaki; later, when the Yamazaki family arrived in Tsurugi at the urging of Tomoshige Fujishima, they joined the already established community of swordmakers there.

No one bothered to reproach Kaho, reduced as he was to making saws and pots, for his version of his family roots. And only local historians even knew of Tomoshige Fujishima. Kaho's daughter, Chigiri, was the only one who could imagine the source of inner strength that kept her father's aging face from softening. Indeed it grew more intensely commanding as the years wore on.

When it came to life taking on unexpected hues, however, Chigiri Yamazaki was the winner.

Not only had she been the main victim of Kaho's stubborn spirit and inability to drop an idea; she had also inherited the traits. The ferment of the land rich with its long history had pushed up a flower and it was she.

Chigiri. Her name meant "a thousand paulownia," and there were paulownia planted in great numbers all along the banks of the Tedorigawa and in the gardens of private homes. Each year, through April and into May, the trees were covered in elegant lavender-colored blossoms. Her father had named her in the hopes that she would become beautiful enough to be a gathering of a thousand paulownia. *Chigiru, chigiri*—the sound of the unusual name made sense to people who knew her. It could also signify "pledge" as in "a solemn vow," and moreover "tear" as in "in half." It was gallant and wholesome, but it also gave a hint of the mad passion between men and women, and this suited her—her body, her very skin—but most surely exceeded any intentions her father had when he named her.

In 1981, that is, two years before Kaho's death, already a couple of years had passed since Chigiri—at the peak of her womanhood, two years past the age of forty—returned to her father's home a divorced woman. There was nothing in her looks or demeanor to criticize, but once every evening, Chigiri cursed her unhappy fate. She kept a smile on her face to make sure the curse did not fall on Mayu, her twelve-year-old daughter, all the while muttering to herself:

It was my weakness, my strength, which led me to divorce and back here with Mayu to my father's home. I've got to find a way out of this. God or Buddha, someone tell me how to do it.

As one might guess from the invocation of God and Buddha at the end, the cursing was mild. Her predicament could be solved with money, but there was nothing so difficult for Chigiri as money.

She wanted to put her father in the hospital, but she didn't have the money to do it. Since she was stuck taking care of him at home, she was unable to go out and work, which meant, of course, that the money she had continued to dwindle.

When her mind began going in circles around this obvious piece of logic, her eyes had the same taut bluish glint that her father's betrayed in his sickbed. That glint had struck her ex-husband, the sort of man who could not accept a woman who failed to fit into his realm, as enigmatic, insolent strength. It wasn't as if Chigiri didn't realize it had led to the divorce.

"You choose to laugh over things that matter and to obsess over things that don't," her husband had said, blinking nervously.

"You've found someone you like better than me. What do you expect me to do? But I didn't laugh."

"You did. You laughed at me, mockingly. You haven't even cried."

"Is that what you want? Tears?"

"It annoys me. Your temperament just doesn't make sense."

"I see."

"What do you mean, 'I see'? That look on your face—"

Divorce had been inevitable.

The ailing Kaho lived with Chigiri and Mayu in the neighborhood of Chimori, in the eastern part of Tsurugi, on the Miyama Plateau in the heart of the mountains. Kingengu Shrine was at its foot, and you could look out to the roads winding high in the foothills. The eastern wind blew against the mountain and tripped off its highest cliffs before hitting the ground. Their house was built right in front of that spot, one that got no wind and little snow, but gave the impression of shrinking into itself to avoid both.

It was in the winter of the year of which we speak that Go Imai, a man who would set the direction for the second half of Chigiri's life, arrived in Tsurugi. He had the position of president of a TV production company called Century Union Go. It sounded impressive, but his title commanded a total of seven employees, including the accountant and receptionist. Imai had already seen two of his enterprises go bankrupt. It was with this third try that he was at last on track.

To get an idea of what he looked like, you need to understand that, until his mid-thirties, he had spent about half of each year making documentaries in Africa, the Middle East, the Himalayas, always out-of-the-way places. He never lost his suntan, a dark color that had penetrated deep into his skin, as he continued his projects, now as an independent producer, taking a camera crew into the world at least twice a year. In concert with the ruddy color, his 47-year-old cheeks and eyelids had begun to droop. His cheekbones stood out sharply and he had a pointy chin. His eyes were enormous, and they could ooze out a moist light that entrapped whomever they were looking at. When he was tired, though, they were nothing more than expressionless glass. Whenever his crew noticed this, they whispered among themselves that they had once again caught Go sleeping with his eyes open.

They whispered because they were afraid. They knew Go was not sleeping, but wondering around the jagged edges of the earth in a precarious state he wanted no one to witness. If they called out while he was on some slippery pass, he might lose his footing and they'd lose him for good.

His forehead was broad and his ears stuck out. As tall as he was, his shoulders were narrow, and he was in the habit of smoking while hunched over, making them even narrower. When he laughed, he looked like nothing more than a dimwitted slacker, but it was that slack smile that made him so appealing to both men and women. There was something plaintive in his smiles and looks of embarrassment, as well as in his fatigue and aging appearance.

When people are sailing smoothly forward, they don't look back. Full of things they need to accomplish, they marshal all of their will power, acumen, and foresight, and the next step forward is what they have in mind even if their strategy requires a step backward. The slowing of the pilgrim's progress is usually due to a decline in health, but even without such a problem, seeing or hitting a wall, or espying an eternity of dark ambiguity, can make them want to turn around, in thrall to an obscure anxiety that they've missed something in all that they've seen and tasted, understood and verified.

Go Imai was approaching such a point in the course of his life, but he was as obtuse as the next man regarding the state of his body and soul. He merely thought that he hadn't been to Kanazawa in a while, that Tsurugi was close by, and that his first shoot at his old production company had been in that town, a quarter-century ago.

Right now he was working on a travelogue, investigating the songs and the foods that had spread along on the Japan Sea coast by ships carrying goods from Osaka to Hokkaido. As president of his small company, he paid courtesy calls to the Kanazawa University professor and the cook at the Nagamachi restaurant who had been of assistance to his director. The next day, he decided on the spur of the moment to visit Tsurugi. He had learned that one job could lead him to new ideas for the next, and he decided to follow his professional intuition.

Truth to tell, he was also drawn to Tsurugi by a memory. Twenty-five years ago, working as an assistant director in the fledgling Japanese television industry, Go had been assigned to follow around a swordsmith, and

an eccentric one at that. Plans were constantly being changed and sched-
ules cancelled, and it had been a difficult project for him. The swordsmith
had refused to cooperate with filming during the summer and had made
Go wait for six months.

In those days, there were no more than a few documentaries made, and
it wasn't unusual to spend a year on one. These days, the entire process,
right through to editing, was allotted no more than two months. It made
Go think about the changes he'd experienced in the ways time and energy
were expended.

He stopped at the station to buy a ticket for an afternoon train to
Tokyo, and then hailed a taxi.

"What part of Tsurugi?" the driver asked.

"The center. Just head for the center."

Then Go, drowsy after a late night of hard drinking, dozed off. In
his semi-conscious state, he saw a tree. Not a pine but a cedar, but it didn't
look like a cedar, with its gnarled roots crawling over the ground. It had
branches growing out of those roots to make a thick shade. A girl in a
sailor-suit-style school uniform sat on one of the branches, watching Go.
Her mouth was twisted self-consciously, but her eyes were bright with
curiosity and yearning. Go aimed the still camera he had for PR shots,
and his finger was on the shutter. The sun coming through the branches
dappled her face, and in the few seconds it took for it to pass, he had
indulged in a few lewd fantasies about the girl set in the square frame.

"By the center, I mean, the center of the fields," Go spoke to his driver.
"Isn't there a famous, old cedar tree somewhere around there?"

"Like at a shrine or a temple?"

"No, there's this cedar, right in the middle of a field. It's famous for
something."

"For what?"

"I think it used to be a mound that belonged to a samurai. You must know that the name Tsurugi has to do with swords and not cranes, don't you?"

"No, I can't say I do."

"The tree had something to do with that."

Go was mistaken. The tree he suddenly decided he had to see again was called the Rokuro Cedar; it had grown wild on the burial mound of a samurai named Hayashi Rokuro-Mitsuaki, who had conquered the region during the Genji-Heike era. It had nothing directly to do with swords. Go's quarter-century-old recollections of Tsurugi history, the swordsmith, and the girl in the sailor suit overlapped like flowers pressed between the pages of a used book.

"Tsurugi has the Hakusan Hime Shrine," said the driver.

"That's right. And Kingengu, too."

"So where is that famous cedar you have in mind?"

"I don't know—it's in a field."

"Lots of houses have cedars, you know."

"It's not a house. All it is is the one tree. Ask someone."

"Do you want to take a picture?"

"Huh, there's snow when you get up this high."

Go had been twenty-two when he'd leered at the girl through the lens with his finger on the shutter. When the TV camera had invaded her home to follow her father around, she had avoided it as if it were a one-eyed monster. After a while, though, she had occasionally eaten take-out lunches with Go and the others, and shown them around town. On the final day of the shoot, they had all gathered under the cedar to take pictures together. As a wrap-up of the program, the girl's father had stood with the tree behind him and talked about the area which had been caught in so many battles during the Age of Warring States and what it had all meant for the swordmakers. The man had a gallant air about him when he wielded his mallet, but as soon as the camera was running, his expression became stiff and his voice tight. The final scene was cut when the documentary was edited. The memories came back as the tires of the taxi crunched over the snow on the road.

As soon as they crossed the Tsurugi town line, Go had the driver stop at a farmhouse, but directions to a spot that could be described as nothing more than an old cedar yielded nothing. It wasn't long before they ended up in the center of town. The inn Go had stayed in during his trips back and forth to Tsurugi was long gone, but the sake brewery and other shops were just about as he had remembered them. He had the taxi wait while he went into the brewery to buy a small bottle of the liquor it was known for. As he accepted his purchase across the solid old counter, he told the proprietor how he had been here long ago to report on a swordmaker and was wondering what had happened to the blacksmith shops in town.

"You mean Kaho Yamazaki, don't you?"

"That's right! That's the one." Once he heard the father's name, he quickly, and somewhat guiltily, recalled that the daughter's name was Chigiri. "He closed shop long ago and moved to Chimori. I'm pretty sure he lives there with his daughter and granddaughter, but he might have died by now." Yamazaki had been over sixty when the documentary was filmed, so this was a possibility Go had already considered.

What was it that made Go decide to continue on to Chimori rather than head back to Kanazawa? It could have been the extra time he had, the weather, a sudden impulse, or a combination of all three. You might even call it fate; you could also chalk it up to Go Imai's tenacity to never go home empty-handed. It was a disposition that had kept him firmly rooted in the television industry. Go went back to the taxi.

"Isn't Chimori somewhere around here? There might be someone there who can tell me where that tree is."

At that moment, the clouds parted to let in a bit of sunlight. The street was deserted and the contours of the houses softened with the easing of the shadows. The only sign of the harsh northland winter was the snow piled up on either side of the road. Water running down the mountains was piped along all the roads, from major arteries to the tiniest of alleys, to help melt the snow. This kept the asphalt shiny black all winter long.

Chimori was an old part of town with houses built closely together along narrow roads. Go saw a sign for a place called Boat Arrival. There must have been a mooring spot for boats sailing up the river. He wondered if the Tedorigawa had originally come as far inland as the cliff he could see in the mountains. He could almost imagine boats waiting at the foot of a long stairway down from Kingengu that came as far as the river, although there was nothing to indicate that such had been the case.

The taxi drove to where the road ended at the entrance to the shrine, backed up into the snow bank, and made a U-turn towards Chimori. Just as the driver was searching for the narrow entrance into the area, Chigiri Yamazaki was backing her tiny car into the garage next to her house. You could call it a garage, but during the winter it also served as home to the clothesline and snow shovels. It had originally been built to store bicycles, and when Kaho had moved there, he had kept all his tools in it. When Chigiri came home after her divorce with a car, the first thing he had done was clear out his own things and pour a concrete floor.

Chigiri had known she'd need a car if she moved back to Tsurugi and she had stubbornly maintained possession of it. Indeed, it had not been long before it became a necessity for taking her father to his doctor's appointments.

She had just got back from one of them and finished bundling her father into the house. Putting the little car into reverse, and turning around to back it in, she was surprised to find the taxi directly behind her. Passing on the narrow lane piled high with snow on both sides was out of the question. The taxi would just have to wait until she had finished parking.

She got out of the car, grabbing the muffler her father had left there, and locked the car door—though she thought it unnecessary in these parts—and headed for the entrance to the house. She was surprised to find the taxi, which she had thought would have long been on its way, stopped.

Chigiri wondered if the passenger was looking for Kingengu. The only taxis she ever saw in her neighborhood were either being used as makeshift ambulances or by the owner of the confectionery a few doors down when he went to Matsuto on business.

She put on a blank expression reserved for anything unnerving or out of the ordinary and began to walk into the house. But the passenger in the taxi got out, and she looked at him, as if asking what he might be doing there.

He wore a black turtleneck sweater and a light brown trench coat with the front open. At that instant, the ray of sun crept back behind a cloud, and for a second the cold air on the road was palpable. The remaining light was behind the man, giving him an overall dark gray appearance that was frightening. Chigiri instinctively stiffened into a defiant stance.

Since her divorce, Chigiri had been reluctant to have dealings with men she didn't know. She knew she had to be careful of herself. The divorce had been her husband's fault, but she suspected that she was the one who had forced him into the indiscretion. A defiant attitude was the only way she knew to protect herself and avoid further unpleasantness, and she was displeased and a little sad to see how hard she had become in the past two years.

As for what she looked like, Go would recall this moment over and over. His fantasies would add details and they would be smudged with fingerprints from his fondling of them, until eventually her expression and actions would become, in his mind, far different from the actuality. He managed to remember correctly what she was wearing. She herself recalled this detail, so he knew he had not been mistaken. He described it as a luscious, chocolate brown dress with a rounded collar that softly described the curves underneath. For Chigiri, it was an old, brown knit dress that she had owned for years. It was warm, that much she could say for it, but she had designated it as a uniform to wear when caring for her father.

Go's fantasies repaired Chigiri's worn features. To him the tight concentration of eyebrows and tiny eyes in the center of her face made her look youthful and innocent. But once she had regained her composure and finally looked up at him, he distinctively sensed a seductive nature that struck him as vaguely dangerous.

Chigiri, of course, was completely unaware of this impression. Nor did she know that, even when she was confused and defenseless, the white glint of teeth barely visible from between her full lips had the power to silence a man. The high-minded airs she gave off made it clear to men that they were in no way allowed to reciprocate the sexuality she exuded, and this in turn deprived her of the opportunity to learn of the effect she had on them.

And what was true for her facial expression also went for the rest of her figure. For example, she was oblivious of the way the brown dress hugged her slim waist, the soft flesh of her back, and showcased the firm muscles of her backside, and from there, the ripe curves of her thighs and legs. Then there was her voice. The more offhanded and gruff she tried to sound the higher and more nasal it became.

"Are you looking for someone's house?"

Chigiri glared suspiciously at Go. She had no way of knowing that the dimwitted yet imposing stance he was taking with her was involuntary. He was waiting with a look of blank amazement on his face as he tried to pull something of great nostalgia from the depths of his memory. Chigiri stared at him with ever-growing suspicion.

"Excuse me?" she prodded sharply.

"Is this the home of Kaho Yamazaki?"

"Yes."

"So you must be his daughter."

"That's right."

"I'm sure you don't remember me."

Chigiri's eyes had finally grown used to the light behind Go, and she took a step toward him and got a good look at his face.

"Well, I'll be."

"Come on, I know you don't remember me."

"I do. You're from the TV company."

He quickly gave his name to avoid the pain of her uttering a misremembered one. It wouldn't have been something to feel hurt over, but he'd hardly paused. If she'd forgotten his name, he wanted her to relearn it—he was Go Imai, from back then.

"That's right. Mr. Imai." It took only an instant for her to feel like she was back in high school.

"Are you sure you remember which one I was? Not the director, but the greenhorn assistant."

"You gave my father a haircut with your electric razor."

"Did I?"

"Yes, he gave you a dagger he had made in return."

"I remember the dagger. That was for a haircut?"

"Otherwise why would he have given something so valuable to the greenhorn assistant?"

When she used the words, it brought him up short, and he searched her expression to see what she meant. It took no more than a few seconds for her cheeks to flush and a smile to appear on her face. Her lips softened, and all of a sudden she was treating him like an old friend. Go was wrapped in a soft, fluffy feeling, of happiness. He felt as familiar with her beautifully shaped lips as if he had already touched them over and over with his fingers and his own mouth.

Somewhere inside Go, he felt a sweet restlessness. A sweat brought broke out on his forehead and neck, although years of dealing with this had taught him how to cover up his excitement.

"You sure have grown up," he said, trying to act calm until he realized how ridiculous it must have sounded. "I mean, not grown up, but grown beautiful. Um, no, how should I put this?"

"I was still in high school."

"And you were very pretty then too."

Chigiri finally broke out in a laugh that enveloped her eyes and cheeks and lips. Go had worked himself into an awkward corner, which Chigiri seemed to be enjoying.

"So you're here to see my father?"

"Uh, yes, and how is he?"

"Not well at all."

"I'm sorry, I just came out on a whim."

He finally told her that his search for the cedar had brought him to her home. Chigiri picked up the muffler she'd dropped in the snow and indicated her surprise that he'd remembered the Rokuro Cedar.

"I looked around in the area where I thought it should be, but couldn't find it."

"Why not stop in for a few minutes. I'll take you there. You might as well get rid of the taxi before the meter goes any higher."

Her decision on the matter had a high-handed attraction to it, and it hit Go like a silken whip. The truth was, though, that even Chigiri was surprised at the way she had ordered him into action. *I'm being self-centered,* she thought. *But self-centered is fine. This man won't chide me.*

Chigiri took Go at face value and continued on in the way of a child used to getting her own way.

"It'll be easier to go there than to try to give you directions. That driver would never be able to find that tiny road through the rice fields. So pay him and come on inside."

If Go had had a hint of perplexity or offense in his eyes, Chigiri would have shifted her gaze. But he drank in both her look and her words, the hint of a flutter in his chest.

For the first time in ages she felt confidence in herself. She felt him accepting everything about her, and she felt herself standing straighter.

Hinomiko, the neighborhood where Rokuro Cedar was located, was actually somewhat distant—nor was it too difficult to give directions to—but Go was delighted with Chigiri's order. He loved women who were direct. During his career in television he had met countless women who had insisted on sulking, those who had flirted with him, and others who had flaunted their power over him with a domineering attitude. Hardly ever did he run into a woman who put only what she had in her heart—everything she had in her heart—into her voice and gaze and send it directly his way.

He didn't want Chigiri to regret her behavior or begin to vacillate, so he did exactly as she said.

"Okay, I'll be right with you." He reached into the back seat of the cab for his bag, paid the driver, watched it leave, and then turned back to Chigiri.

"Excuse me," she said hurriedly, "would you mind waiting out here a few moments?"

She ran to the entrance, pulled open the sliding glass door, and then closed it behind her. Go realized she probably wanted to straighten up the house. He mentally kicked himself for not being more perceptive, wishing he had said he'd like to take a walk around the neighborhood. As for Chigiri, she didn't know how to make the house any neater. She pulled out some cushions and rearranged them a few times.

Go walked towards the garage. The tiny blue car was a discontinued domestic model. The inside wall was of corrugated plastic, and he could see through a crack in it to the garden. The same plastic had been used to protect the house from snow, so he couldn't see inside, but set in the middle of the tiny garden was an anvil. On top of that was a plate of shredded *mochi* rice cake.

Returning to the entrance, Go noticed the camellia by the garage and the conifers behind the house, their tops almost covering the roof. Both the camellia and the trees were covered in white, the former in full bloom and the latter sprinkled with snow. He realized with a start that something was about to begin. It might be something dull and uninspiring, something he had experienced countless times before, something that wouldn't make a lick of difference when he died. But it was always good to have something about to begin.

He had to laugh at the excitement he felt growing in him, and he wasn't really sure whether he could handle it. He had had it dozens of times, but he couldn't remember which time had been the best, or even the last. *It might be different this time,* he thought fleetingly, but it took no more than a deep breath or two to get that notion out of his head.

A single look from Chigiri had affixed a sticker somewhere in his body that would be impossible to rip off. The flush on her white cheeks, her deeply black, long-slitted eyes. The light in those eyes worked in a remarkable tandem with her lips. The soft but deep smile, the command of her voice that did not trail off, the sweet resonance of her voice that made the listener happy to acquiesce.

Confused, he thought over the sticker that had been slapped on him, and as he was doing so, the glass door slid open and the real Chigiri appeared to interrupt his ruminations, almost to his regret.

"Come on in. We just got back from the doctor's."

"I should have gone for a walk."

"I don't mind. It's a mess, but be my guest. We're as poor as we ever were."

"I love that."

"What's to love?"

"How you said 'poor'; you're a magician. Sounded cheerful as bell."

Chigiri blushed. Now she wanted to say it again, with pride. Like a child, she wanted to say it a hundred times, be praised a hundred times. Embarrassed at herself, she laughed.

2

WHEN YOU CAN SAY ANYTHING you like and don't need to be afraid of eliciting anger; when it's not exactly trust, but there is the relief of being with someone you feel like you've known for years and who understands you: when this happens between two people in the space of a heartbeat, and those two happen to be a man and a woman, it is probably love. The two may avoid using such a word, and even refuse to acknowledge it outside of novels and films, but love it is.

But in Go Imai's case, he felt certain his verbal flinging of the affection that had surely arisen only in him at the woman before him was begging for indulgence, and so he quickly added words to soften the effect.

"When you said 'poor,' it sounded almost refreshing, and there was something clean and healthy about it. I didn't get a sense of poverty."

It made Chigiri want to hide the old shoe rack in the tiny entryway, Kaho's cane covered with the dirt from his hands, Mayu's tired old tennis shoes that had been washed and hung, and her worn-out boots.

The shoe rack's top boasted a single porcelain frog her daughter had received from a friend a while ago. Forget the poor taste, neither money nor energy had been spent on adorning the space. Chigiri's financial concerns had robbed her of the joy of beautifying her home.

"This way," she said to Go, "but please don't be surprised."

The inner sitting room of the house was almost fully occupied by the bedding of the old man. Some sunlight managed to filter through the plastic surrounding the house to guard it from snow. Go felt like he was in an illusion that had him wandering into a paper lantern. Kaho looked like a thin pole of a man wrapped up inside a tiny snow cave. Go hardly recognized him.

"Here is my father. His lungs are bad, and so is his head. I'm sure he doesn't remember you."

It was a sordid scene, but coaxed by Chigiri's cheery voice, Go looked over at the unresponsive old man to find his smart chiseled face intently focused on nothing, like an ancient warrior gazing at a fire in the dark.

"Dad, would you please look at this man?"

As if following a fleck of fire, the man's gaze flew out and landed on Go's face. His mouth moved impatiently, and his eyebrows flexed and then relaxed and then flexed again.

"I see. Thank you very much. I knew we'd be seeing you again."

"Dad?"

"My daughter Chigiri will pay you what we owe. We won't be of any further bother to you. Red pine charcoal is what we need. I can't get on with my work without it."

"This is Mr. Imai from the television company. Do you remember when he came to make the documentary about you?"

"You pay him what we owe."

"You're thinking of someone else." Chigiri put her hand on her father's shoulder and laughed. Go laughed, too, and finally so did Kaho. "Dementia is one of his symptoms. The older you get, the more diseases come around to have fun with you. Right, Dad? You've lived a long life, and that's just the way it works out."

"You're absolutely right." Kaho responded with unruffled dignity, and they all laughed again. Go got the impression she was working magic on the old man, while Chigiri was merely relieved that her father was able to laugh along with Go.

"I did the math in the taxi; it's been twenty-five years since I was here. Your daughter reminded me that I once gave you a haircut. I still have the dagger you gave me for it."

Go was talking to the old man, but he was facing Chigiri. She, in turn, got up to get some tea. Checking the cupboard, there wasn't a teacup worthy of presenting to a guest, so she pulled out a box from deep inside a drawer. It held a white teacup, given out as a commemorative gift when a pickle shop had opened. She unwrapped it and washed it under the tap. She looked around frantically for something to go with the tea, and her eyes landed on a package of stale crackers. She finally grabbed a container of soft dried plums she'd bought for her father. She pulled out one and planted it ceremonially in the middle of a small dish.

"I really hadn't planned on visiting and causing you any trouble. I just came by and your daughter kindly invited me in."

Each time Chigiri, standing in the kitchen, looked back at Go, he averted his eyes. But when she turned her back to pour the tea and set a toothpick next to the plum, she could feel his eyes, starting on her back and making their way down. They were no more than a dozen feet from each other, and Chigiri felt as if the air was full of a particularly thick gelatin in which she needed to move as deliberately as possible. She tried to look quickly over at Go, but found him looking at Kaho's face with a blank expression. Maybe he hadn't been watching her after all.

"Did your mother pass away?"

He must be looking at the photograph over the family altar, realized Chigiri, as she set the teacups on a tray.

"Twelve years ago."

She had the tray in her hands, but looked ruefully at the single plum. *He'll never touch it.*

But she was wrong. Go put his hands together in a gesture of thanks, and popped the red plum into his mouth. Then he reached out for the teacup. Chigiri noticed that he was sitting properly on his knees and quickly encouraged him to stretch his legs out.

She also picked up the coat he had balled up and laid in a corner, and hung it on a hook on the wall. The cloth of the coat felt good, like something she ought not to be touching, she thought. But she wanted to hang it up neatly, hoping to give Go the impression it would be rude to leave too abruptly, although, she reasoned with herself, there was really no reason why she particularly wanted him to stay.

He hadn't been in the house for more than ten minutes. Chigiri pretended to be thinking nostalgically of her mother, instead thinking that it was the first time a man like Go had been in the house. She wasn't exactly sure what she meant by a "man like Go," but he was a being, neither boy nor old man, that had a barrier of odor and provoked a woman to tension.

She sensed the odor with her whole body. It was a disquieting odor that tugged at a string that seemed to stick out of her body.

Chigiri refocused herself on staying calm and reasonable, fighting back the waves crashing inside her. After all, Go Imai had come to see Kaho. She herself astutely kept her eyes on her father to show that she fully understood Go's purpose in visiting them.

"I'm sure it was one of the most exciting times in his life. The old blacksmith was suddenly being heralded as an artist. We had our hands full for a while after the show was aired on TV."

Was he really here just to see her father? She hoped that he had at least a fleeting interest in her. She refused, however, to act needy. Admitting their poverty was one thing, but this was something else.

"He started calling the kids in the neighborhood who helped him out his Number One Apprentice, Number Two Apprentice, and so on." The memory was so funny it made tears roll down her face. "And, and, of course, it was all thanks to you," she finished up with a nod.

The conversation they held with the patient lying between them was limited to the days they'd worked together twenty-five years ago, Chigiri's mother's death, and her father's retirement. During a pause, she had wanted to ask him about his own career, but she didn't want to seem too interested.

"What's that?" Go asked pointing to the shelf of the family's Shinto shrine.

"Where?"

"That, up near the ceiling, over the shrine."

"It's the character for 'cloud.'"

Chigiri had been the one to hang the calligraphy at that spot. Kaho had written it. The ink had run where the rain from a typhoon had leaked in through the eaves.

"Why 'cloud'?"

"There's a second floor over the shrine, and it's not good to have people walking over it. This means that there are nothing but clouds over the shrine."

"Is that some kind of rule?"

"That's right. It's a rule. Once it's decided, everything's a lot easier. Now we can walk over that spot as much as we like."

"I see."

"The gods can't scold us for anything that goes on on the second floor. Does that sound unusual to you?"

"It's a piece of wisdom. I love it. A rule."

Chigiri's eyes met Go's. At that moment she was convinced that Go had not come in merely to see her father, but to see her, too. She was flustered to see his slightly droopy eyes that seemed to gush warm feelings, and no longer hid her agitation. She returned the look and swallowed hard. She began to move her lips, but then firmly closed them.

"Now that you mention it, Kaho had a number of rules that he followed, too. There were all of those different ceremonies he followed while forging a sword. That was interesting."

"It must have been practical to follow procedures in a certain way, to yield a better finish," suggested Chigiri. It had been so long ago. She didn't recall her father striking the steel in his white work clothes as a beautiful ceremony. She had seen him as a blacksmith taking care of business in his own particular way. The television program had presented Kaho as a venerable craftsman of the old school, and Kaho himself had been dissatisfied with the illusion it created.

"The world of TV has no rules, well, very few, and the ones we have are always changing. It can be a liability sometimes."

"So have you stayed in the television business?"

"The documentary we made here was my first one, and I've been doing the same thing ever since." He handed Chigiri his card.

"My! You're the president."

"I couldn't even guess how many hundreds of little companies like mine flood the industry. No matter how many go under, there are always more to replace them."

"It sounds like fun."

At the time, the "cloud" on the ceiling was no more than an old custom, a blurred and faded Chinese character. Neither of them could have imagined that some rule like that could constrain or even upset a person's life. *Let's just say that that's the way it is.* Rules were good for sorting things out, and once they were sorted out and neatly stored in the rule box, you could conveniently get lots of other things in there too. But these "things" were often people's hearts, and once the heart had been made to conform to a "way it is," it could quickly grow to hate it.

"Did it have to be 'cloud'? It couldn't have been 'sky' or 'star'?"

Go regretted his words the moment he spoke. Without the passion to select words with some eye to a point, jokes merely wounded their utterer. Perhaps he had always been making lame jokes. Perhaps all he'd really done for the past twenty-five years was to earn his living by throwing sundry images and words up on the tube: if clouds didn't do, then the sky; sky no good, then stars.

If so, his body was covered in wounds. He simply hadn't noticed.

Watching him grow pensive, Chigiri felt ill-at-ease with Go for the first time since he'd arrived.

In the following years, some houses were built nearby, but in 1981, the Rokuro Cedar stood alone in a snow-covered field, a small forest unto itself. There was only the one tree, but its roots were divided into several arteries, and branches had grown twisted and horizontal to the ground.

Cedars are trees that, when left on their own, grow straight towards the sky. For this tree to have grown in this particular shape, some force must have come into play. With the river, Tedorigawa, close by, there could have been a flood that uprooted it, only to have it take root and continue growing on its side. Or there could have been wind. Judging from its size, the chances that it was around during the days of Hayashi Rokuro-Mitsuaki were slim. It couldn't be more than a hundred or a hundred-and-fifty years old.

A cedar that was merely old or that had a thick trunk would not draw attention to itself, but rarely if ever did one come across a cedar that looked like this, crawling across the ground as it was. And it had grown on the mound of an old samurai from the Genji-Heike era. That was interesting, too. There was something about the tree that contradicted the samurai spirit, and it had the effect of bringing the owner of the mound closer to one's heart.

"I remember this shape, but the trunk and branches have gotten even thicker since then."

Go spoke thus as he took a slow turn around the tree. The snow on the surface had begun to melt in the sun before it froze up again for the night. He felt it crunching beneath his feet.

"Very few people know about this tree, even in Tsurugi. Why did you decide to use it in the documentary?"

"I don't remember," admitted Go. "It was the director who made the decision. He said it reminded him of Kaho, standing out there alone in the cold and the wind. All I can remember are these branches."

"Me too."

"This was the last place."

"No, it wasn't. The last part was my father putting some old scrolls back into the drawers of the family altar.

"Not the end of the program; this was the last place we filmed."

"Was it?"

"We even took a group picture to commemorate the occasion. Chigiri, you were wearing your school uniform, and you sat right over there."

Go pointed to a comfortable looking branch, one that was black with the moisture of the snow. There, he'd referred to her by her first name, and she didn't seem to mind.

"Shall we sit there again?" she suggested.

"It's all wet."

"I'm fine with that."

Go considered prefacing his next remark with a "I'm not just being polite when I say" but thought the better of it. He remarked: "I can't believe it's twenty-five years later."

"Well, it is. I went to a junior college, got married, had a child, and got divorced. And this tree has been right here the whole time."

"As ill-mannered as ever."

"Yes, but it's so comfortable."

"How old is your child?"

"She's twelve. How about you, Mr. Imai?"

"I have two sons."

Light and shade played over their faces, and he felt like he could ask and talk about anything he liked. When it came to asking the details of her past, which she had laid out so simply and then set aside, it wasn't as easy as he had thought. There must have been some serious reason behind a beautiful women like her getting divorced. Perhaps her husband had loved her too much and gone mad from the fury of his jealous rages. He knew of a few such cases of self-destruction.

Typically for a man in his situation, Go decided that the divorce had all been the fault of her ex-husband.

Chigiri wanted to talk to him, and it was all she could do to stop herself. She wanted him to know how her husband had been unfaithful and how she had somehow accepted it. It was Mayu who had urged her to leave him, and after she had, her husband had stopped sending them the promised support after a mere six months. She hadn't talked to anyone about it, and she desperately wanted to now, but she was sure it would give away her lack of competence.

"Your daughter must be a help to you."

"She's still only twelve. She always wants this or that. There's always something she needs, and I've got to be both mother and father to her."

"It sounds hard. With your father that way, too. You be sure to let me know if you need money."

Go said it without thinking. It was no more than a social formality, but the sound of it left something like a metallic clink between them. There wouldn't have been the slightest problem if he'd said something more abstract like *Come talk to me if you need help* or *Let me know if there's anything I can do for you*, but he'd specifically said "money."

What Go said next, though, helped to soften the effect: "Anyone who uses the word 'poor' and makes it sound like fun, well, money is the only thing I can use to compete with that."

What he meant was poverty and money were of little significance, and Chigiri seemed to get the point. "So you're rich?"

If she had looked at him with contempt or scorn, their relationship might have headed in a completely different direction. Her eyes betrayed an innocent curiosity more likely to be directed at a rare flower, clock, or piece of clothing rather than money and people who had it.

"No," Go responded, "I've got all kinds of debts."

"You don't say." This so clearly contradicted his offer of help that Chigiri was at a loss as to how to react.

"But I can use money to move things around me. I've got some I can

33

use as I like. In my business, it's like moving water from the bucket in your right hand to the bucket in your left. Some of the water is bound to spill, so you use it to slake your thirst."

"So, you *handle* large amounts of money."

"The buckets come in all different sizes, but all you do is move the water from one to the next, and then back again. I'm always busy making sure of the amounts of the checks and the due dates on the bills. Me and my seven employees are somehow managing to make a living, so I guess we must be making some sort of profit."

Go sat down on the thickest branch, the one farthest away from Chigiri. There was no snow within a few yards of the root; the snow had, instead, fallen on top of the leaves, been melted by the sun, and was now dripping off them.

Chigiri spoke again after a short pause in the conversation.

"The television business. Surrounded by beautiful women and always the vanguard of trendy. Nothing scares you."

"I guess." Go suddenly looked serious. Something was swelling up inside him. "I suppose you're right about being at the vanguard of trendy. But that's not always a pretty place to be. The part about beautiful women, largely true."

"Are you angry at me?"

"I can line up many women, below the waist. Above the shoulders I can't expect much."

"Really?"

"No. Just kidding."

"So you've had a lot of fun with lots of women."

"Me? I guess so. Lots of fun."

Go watched Chigiri's reaction. She looked as confused as a puppy that had dug itself into a deep hole. Go felt a nearly aggressive affection for her that he packed into a brashness of tone for want of other options.

"None of us have a decent home life. We're all too scared to go home and find what's waiting for us there. I never want to look too far ahead either. I just follow whatever is right in front of me. I go for the beef bowl someone's handing me rather than walk three blocks to check out the French cuisine. It's the same with women and money, and that's why I'm always so busy." As soon as he said this, he had to say the next thing flying into his head. "Of course, that's not the way I was twenty-five years ago."

He remembered looking at something higher up and farther away. He had been sure he could convince and impress anyone in the world with his work as long as it was the truth, and as long as it came from deep inside of himself. The trick was to find it and protect it. He had been ready to work for what he wanted.

"Aren't you cold?" Chigiri asked.

"Yeah."

"Shall we go?"

"No, not yet. I finally made it here, can't we stay a little longer?"

As soon as he said *a little longer*, his body jolted. He wanted to pull Chigiri into his arms, and press his cheek against hers. She'd certainly be flustered, but he wanted to feel the weight and warmth of her body. He wanted to start at the lobe of her ear with his lips and slowly move across her face till he reached her lips. He felt her reaction in his arms as soon as he imagined this.

He forcefully ripped his gaze from her lips; his breathing was rough. *What do I have here?* he wondered. You could say he had made his way through the rough breakers of life, he knew about reality, he had learned about life, he was old and depraved. But no, it was none of that. What he had was a quiet, yet hot mass of emotion. It was time; it was what he had gained from time. If you had to call it something, he whispered to himself as he tried to calm his breathing, it was a thin film of sadness. Thin, but absolute in its sadness.

It was then that Go was surprised to discover that he could still be moved by this sort of emotion. It wasn't just sexual desire. It was a painful throb from higher up, from his chest, that worked its way down into desire.

Was it this tree, or was it this woman who had suffered so much and yet seemed so fresh and pure? He hadn't suffered through the last twenty-five years, no, but he hadn't felt this way in quite a while.

Go cleared his throat. "I have to admit, I'm a dyed-in-the-wool TV man. You can knock me over or blow me off, but I won't get back up without something in my hand. I thought I might find something in Tsurugi. At the very least, I'd get a bottle of beautiful sake to take back to Tokyo with me."

"Nothing's changed, has it, in town?"

"I always come up with something, but sometimes it's the most curious thing."

Go looked at Chigiri. He couldn't go on any further. Chigiri was unable to grasp exactly what he meant. Her heart was beating and she was holding her hands together so tightly the tips went hard as wood. She wished he would be more clear about his intentions, and she waited.

"Would you mind if I called you when I got back to Tokyo?"

"Not at all."

"May I come back here again?"

Chigiri put her strength into her lips and then let them slowly loose to laugh awkwardly. "Of course not. What is there for you to do here?"

Regretting how cold it sounded, she quickly dipped her head in apology.

Go said he'd get a cab from Tsurugi Station, but Chigiri volunteered to drive him back to Kanazawa. She assured Go that Mayu should be home from school and could look after things for a few hours, and he accepted.

The traffic signals grew more frequent as they approached Kanazawa. Once they crossed the Saigawa, the bustle of evening was evident in town.

"I wish I could stay another night."

Chigiri did not respond to Go's muttering. She thought again about what he'd said about "lots of fun" and reminded herself that he was going back to a place that offered a lot more excitement than Kanazawa.

Chigiri drove through Katamachi and Korinbo, and arrived at Kanazawa Station more quickly than she'd imagined. They barely said a word of parting, one inside the car and the other outside, ducking their heads in a quick bow and going their separate ways.

On the way home, Chigiri realized later, her behavior was disconnected and illogical. She called home to make sure Mayu was there, and then stopped in at a bookshop in Matsuto to buy a weekly tabloid. She stayed to browse through a book on fortune-telling before putting it back on the shelf. Her next stop was a cosmetics shop where she got some fragrance and hair spray, and then impulsively bought some underthings. As the clerk wrapped up the cream-colored lacy panties she had chosen, she wondered aloud whether her daughter would like them, knowing full well they weren't the sort of thing girls in sixth grade would be caught dead in changing in and out of gym clothes.

Her shopping finished, Chigiri still did not head straight home, but stopped at the Tengu Bridge on the Tedorigawa, and walked down to the snow-covered riverside.

The river flowing towards the sun in the west looked almost warm, and despite the cold she felt, she squatted down and flipped through the pages of the magazine. There wasn't a thing in it she was interested in, and the light wasn't really bright enough for her to read the print.

She closed the magazine and put her hands to her knees. "God and Buddha," she said. It was the same incantation she mouthed whenever she felt anxious, but she could not formulate a concrete request and so called the names of the deities three times each before finally coming up with something she thought she could ask for.

God and Buddha, please make sure Mr. Imai never comes near me again.

Realizing that her wish might come true, and certain that it wasn't what she really wanted, she asked for something else as well. *He said he'd call, and a phone call wouldn't be so bad. If I just heard his voice, that might not be a problem, so please make sure he calls.*

The day's doings could only be described as a calamity in Chigiri's life. She couldn't escape, nor would things end up as she wanted. Once she was dragged into the situation, she wouldn't easily be free of it. Anything as treacherous as the course of events as she imagined them would be a calamity for her. She could ignore it all, and if that were impossible, she'd have to turn him down flat, anything to be done with it all as soon as possible. Still, she knew in her heart that it was more likely that her father would recover from his illness, that money would fall from the sky, or that she'd suddenly be ten years younger.

Imai's eyes as they watched her, his lightly closed lips, the soft yet heavy voice that came out of them, the way he cleared his throat, the movement of his chest, the small of his back, the round swell of his backside, all of him flooded Chigiri's thoughts, filling every nook and cranny, just like the flash of a camera. Her mind had stopped working, and she shook from the violent sweetness of it all.

No one had touched her in the two years since her divorce. She was sure that was the cause.

Chigiri tried giving such a name to the calamity.

He'd never call her. That was how things went. She'd find clarity in a couple of years, or maybe even six months.

As if in support of this prediction, she stared determinedly over at the other side of the river, stood up and went back to her car.

3

THREE DAYS AFTER HE'D got back from Tsurugi, Go Imai was in Akasaka, in an expensive hotel with a girl who was taking her clothes off. He sat sunk in a chair, watching the scene as if it had nothing to do with him, but he could tell she was embarrassed. Three hours before, the president of a production company had introduced her to him, but at twenty-three she seemed just a little too old to be playing the role of up-and-coming.

The girl was completely naked, and gave Go a questioning look. "Aren't you going to take off your clothes?"

"Oh yeah, sorry."

"Should I take a shower first?"

"Do whatever you like."

"I've got a condom."

"Fine."

"It's kind of hot; do you mind if I turn down the heat?"

"Go ahead. You've got nice boobs."

He took off his pants and briefs, and when he was down to his T-shirt, he moved over to the bed. He wasn't heading for the shower, and he didn't roll over either. He was a middle-aged man sitting on the edge of the bed, and the girl stood there trying to decide what to do next.

"I don't need sex."

"But…"

"You should do that with someone you like."

"Don't you like me?"

"Use your hand or your mouth, put on the condom if that would be easier."

"I'm not really good at that."

"I haven't had a woman in a while, it won't take long."

"You want it like this?"

"Your ass, from here your backbone looks like a railroad track running up to two white mountains. Soft and round. Okay, now it feels good. Put the condom on."

Just when he began to feel bad about all the work she was putting into it, he ejaculated towards the two white mountains. He didn't have his old stamina, and he mumbled to himself about what he was capable of.

"You were great," he reassured the girl.

"Are you sure?"

"Did the boss tell you to do it? Don't worry, I'll find you some work. When you ate that atrocious tuna at dinner, you made it look like it tasted wonderful. You'll be good on travel programs."

"The tuna was atrocious?"

"Just do your best on the shoot; just make it look fun."

"I'll do my best!"

"You might have to fix the way you hold chopsticks."

"I'm not good with my hands. I can't even get this off right."

Go watched her pull off the condom and then stuff it into a wad of tissue so it wouldn't spill. He smiled at her cheerful chatter, and laughed. He was glad he hadn't gone through and slept with her.

Better still, when the president of the production company had slipped the key into his hand and suggested, between courses at dinner, that he get some rest, he could have turned him down and gone on home.

Serves me well! Proof it's been twenty-five years since Tsurugi.

His office was less than a ten-minute walk from the hotel, on the sixth floor of a building of condominiums. For some reason each and every "residence" had a sign by the door with the name of a company. His camera crew and editor had been there when he'd left, but they were all gone now. He decided the time was right. Now that he'd lost some of that excess sexual energy, he might be able to talk to her without sounding too sentimental.

Serves me well.

He tried to get back that instant of liberation by rolling his head and shrugging his shoulders a few times. Then he sighed and looked at the clock. You couldn't say it was the middle of the night. It was just a little before eleven. It still wasn't an unreasonable hour.

For the past quarter-century, Go Imai had worked until two or three in the morning and could go for days without ever going home. For him, eleven at night was just this side of reasonable. For Chigiri, who had a child and an invalid to care for, it was indeed the middle of the night, with her day done, all hopes and expectations neatly folded up and put away.

For her part, Chigiri had decided early that evening that she was not going to be hearing from Go. She had waited and waited the previous two nights and been severely disappointed. Her irritation with the part of herself that still thought he might call had peaked, and she had forced herself to give up on him altogether.

She'd convinced herself that giving up was usually the best way to make things happen. Things often came out of nowhere as soon as you stopped looking for them, and wasn't there a song about that?

She was certain she was done with the thought of Go for good, but she really wasn't. Once you had fallen into a trap, you couldn't make it go away by ignoring it. When the phone rang, she picked it up after first reminding herself it must be a wrong number, and out of the receiver came Go's voice.

"Were you in bed?"

"Yes. I mean no. I'm still up."

"I had planned to call as soon as I got back to Tokyo, but I was busy." It wasn't a lie, but it was a line men often used. Being busy with work was mostly an excuse, but sometimes it served as a badge to give a man substance. Right now, Go was using it to cover up his true feelings, but he wasn't quite cool enough to avoid blowing his cover.

"I mean, well, I was busy, but the truth is that I didn't have the courage to call."

"Courage?"

"I haven't needed courage to make a call for years and years. That's why..." Go knew he was in trouble now, but he sounded so bold that he gave Chigiri the impression that he used this sort of tactic all the time.

"So, are you still in the process of building up your courage?"

"Exactly."

"You sound like you're used to it."

"To what?"

"Making courageous phone calls. I don't think it's been all that long since you made one."

Go wanted to insist that he meant it, but he stopped himself. He might as well be the man she thought she was talking to.

"Well, every man could always use some courage when he calls a woman."

"Always?"

"Of course. It makes sense when it's a woman you like, doesn't it?"

Words, they were eluding his control. His own words were betraying him, building up a different him. He panicked. He wasn't really in a state to be bandying phrases like "a woman you like."

The line was silent. He fearfully waited for her voice to come back donning the same cool disdain he saw dancing on her face. The actual facial expression on the woman, however, was somewhat different from what the man pictured. She'd been paralyzed by the words "a woman you like."

For the past few days, she had created a figure of Go Imai, the playboy who had "a lot of fun with women." She had used it to protect herself from disappointment, and perhaps that mechanism had exaggerated the image. He'd told her that he had all the female companionship he needed. That was the sort of life he led.

Yet, when the frank declaration came, she was rendered speechless.

"What's the matter?"

"Nothing. You *are* irresponsible."

"I'm telling the truth. And I forgot to thank you for driving me all the way to Kanazawa. How is your father?"

"He's still reminding me to pay you back those loans."

"Well, I just might take a trip back to Tsurugi to pay back some of those loans for you. Are there men hanging around looking for their money?"

"Of course. I told you we were poor."

"I don't think I can let you get away with being such a cheerful pauper." Go could hear her laughing lightly.

"I'm not as cheerful as you think."

"You're lovely. I can see you smiling. I can see your lips. The skin around your eyes is just slightly pink. I'm right, aren't I?"

"I'm in the kitchen, and there's no mirror for me to check. But you might be right."

"Of course I am. You've got to let me go back to Tsurugi and pay off your debts."

"Even if you come, there might not be anyone to pay; and why do you have to pay anyway?"

"So who do you owe money to?"

"To the man who sells us steel and to our relatives. We haven't paid for the flat iron or the rods, either. It's been years."

"Then you've got to pay."

"The steel place went out of business and the boss died quite a while back. We've got debts from twenty years ago, but nobody to pay them back to. That's the way things go."

"The statute of limitations has come and gone, I guess."

"I just wish my father's memory had a statute of limitations."

"I'll have to go!"

Chigiri was silent. Go was doing his best to come up with a reason to get to Tsurugi; there was no denying it.

"Let me help you with your debts," he tried again.

"What?"

"I don't mean I'll help you make more; I mean I can help you pay them back."

"But why?"

Go felt like he had a blade pressed against his throat. He had to say something at that point. What he was about to blurt out would have reverberations for months to come. It just came out, like some self-effacing reflex, but was not something he could have ever said to Chigiri's face.

In a voice that was even clearer and calmer than hers, he replied, "There's only one reason. I want you. You're what I'm after."

He was still tipsy. But he was momentarily wrapped in a desperate darkness in which he cursed himself again. It was the collapse following his tension and hesitation.

He hastily tried to rephrase himself.

"Now I've done it again. Don't be mad, I'm just no good at making jokes anymore. It's age."

It hadn't been a joke, nor had it been exactly what he meant. It was the sort of rude comment men often made to women, and there was usually an element of truth in it.

Go tried to imagine Chigiri's kitchen. He tried to remember where the phone had been. He had sat next to Kaho and looked through the doorway to the kitchen. He was fairly sure the phone had been quite a distance from Kaho's bedside, and was relieved at the recollection. But in the next instant he recalled what he had just said and his face went hot with embarrassment.

"Are you mad at me? I'm sorry. Ever since I met you again in Tsurugi, I've had this notion that I could say anything to you and you'd forgive me. And I'm a little drunk. But I didn't call you just to mess around. Just the opposite."

"It's all right. I'd appreciate your help."

"What?"

"I'm saying that if you lend me some money, you can have me."

"Come on, don't be angry."

"I'm not. I'm not upset at all."

"I'm going to see you to apologize."

"I don't need your apology, I need—"

"What do you need?"

"I need the money. I'm asking you for a loan. We don't owe the relatives much, but I want my father in the hospital. His lung cancer is getting worse, and I can't just leave him like this. But I can't make any money unless he's being cared for somewhere else."

Now Go went quiet. Chigiri had rattled her saber at him, and his drunken haze was gone in a flash. He was stunned by the sudden turn in the conversation.

"How, how much do you need?"

"I don't know."

"Why don't you know?"

"Look, you're the one that brought up the subject and I'm no good at numbers. I take after my father like that."

"All right then, I'll see what I can come up with, and you'll have to make do with it."

"Thank you."

"Today too, I slept with a woman I'd met for the first time. A man who runs a third-rate production company showed up with her. I'm that sort of fool. So you've got nothing to worry about."

Go was at a loss, and he knew nothing he said was making sense.

"Please don't worry, is what I meant. I promise this won't become anything, you know, heavy for you."

All Go heard in response was the sound of her breathing.

"What I mean—" Go tried to add a word, but Chigiri broke in.

"About that woman."

"Yes?"

"That woman."

"Who?"

"The one tonight. Was she charming?"

"Oh. Um, I was lying. I didn't really sleep with her."

Now Chigiri was totally confused. A feeling that was neither mirth nor sorrow filled her bosom. She was pretty sure he wasn't mocking her, but that was all she was sure of."

"I didn't sleep with her. That was a lie."

"All I asked was, was she charming?"

"I can't even remember what she looked like. Doesn't that show you what kind of a man I am? You've got nothing to worry about."

Chigiri had to laugh. There was no force in it, and it sounded both uneasy and a little angry. But it was really the only thing the situation called for, so she had laughed.

"Don't try too hard to come up with the money."

"No, please don't scrap our deal. It's all been decided. I'll get together some money that you won't need to pay back."

Chigiri's laughter died down, and Go no longer heard anything on the other end of the phone. Then she spoke in a quiet, but clear voice.

"You're right. It'll probably be easier if we work out a relationship that involves payments."

Go didn't know what she meant. Even Chigiri wasn't sure why it would be easier that way. She wanted to believe that it was because she needed the money. Nothing more.

Now Chigiri was just as guilty as Go of trying to cover her tracks after a gush of rare emotion. The best way to avoid being overwhelmed by such a flow was to channel it in another direction. Chigiri, then, did so out of instinct.

After she hung up, the first thing Chigiri did was go into the next room to make sure her father was asleep. Then, she climbed partway up the stairs to make sure Mayu hadn't been listening in. Everything was quiet. She went into the tiny room off the kitchen and lied down on the sofa bed they had moved out of the living room to make room for her father's bed; it was where she spent her nights.

She had to go over the conversation she had just had. The words Go had spoken to her sped around inside her head, jumping from side to side. They took up all the available space. *I want you. You're what I'm after. I'm just no good at making jokes anymore. I'm going to see you to apologize. I slept with a woman I'd met for the first time. I'm that sort of fool. So you've got nothing to worry about.*

The words refused to settle down. She couldn't digest them or throw them up. She turned over and over on the bed. The only thing she was sure of was that both Go Imai and his money were headed in her direction and that she was bound to be hurt pretty deeply were she to resolve to be happy about the prospect.

Go, too, was confused. The phone call had him heading down a slippery slope. He was confused, but that didn't keep him from moving ahead. He went over to the desk of the woman who did his office work and switched on her computer. He checked his company's accounts. Then he went to his own desk and unlocked the bottom drawer. He took out a wad of about a dozen bankbooks bound together with rubber bands. He had a few bills that he was waiting for payment on, and some drafts that were dated a few months ahead. He put them all out on the desk. Most of the broadcasting company drafts were dated a few months ahead, and part of those sums needed to go to paying freelance directors, cameramen, and editors. His assistant deposited the largest drafts in the safe at the bank, but smaller or nearly due ones were kept in his desk drawer.

Half of the bankbooks had balances of zero. Some were in his name, others were in the company's name, still others were in the name of the accountant who had worked for him for years before quitting. He had handed them back to Go along with the stamp seal he needed to withdraw the balance. It was money that was his to do with as he pleased. There was a large amount, but he had kept it on hand for emergencies.

He had promised to get some money for her without knowing how much she needed. Nor did he know how much of what he had he could safely give her.

What price lust?

It was easier for him to think of it that way rather than as love.

He didn't realize it, but he had a bad habit of calling on his vulgar side whenever he shied away from his emotions. It was the only way he felt safe. He muttered "lust, lust," busily stomping on the flutter in his heart. In a way, apart from the masculine excitement over access to Chigiri's body, this chanting was a frank expression of joy that he could come up with a way to help her.

Society would certainly interpret the scene as Chigiri caught in Go's trap. But Go, sputtering on about his lust, was more likely the helpless beast caught in a sweet trap and strung up high, a forty-seven-year-old man who was wondering about losing himself.

4

FROM ALL APPEARANCES, IN A single phone call Go Imai had agreed to provide Chigiri with money in exchange for sex. In actuality, no action was taken on the matter for the next month-and-a-half. Go had the money and was ready to leave for Tsurugi on a moment's notice, but just as he had feared, Chigiri was balking.

"I don't think this is such a good idea."

"If you insist on labeling it good or bad, of course it's bad."

"I'm not suggesting we quit because it's bad."

"It's not good, but it is. I can't explain why over the phone."

Chigiri laughed, and Go was relieved at the sign that she didn't hate him.

"Once again: it's not because I want you that I prepared the sum."

"You just want me to accept it."

"That's right."

"So you've said, Mr. Imai, but what good would it do you then?"

"Please don't call me that."

"What would be in it for you, Go?"

That moment, the two of them had quite disparate words in mind. Chigiri was certain the only good for Go was sex but wasn't even sure she was good for him. As for Go, he was anxious to tell her he wasn't just interested in her body but never got around to it. He wanted her to know it wasn't his only motivation, but he did want to sleep with her after all.

"I won't force you to do anything you don't want to. I promise."

"I can still scrape by with what we've got."

"So you hate me?"

"No."

"So it's the money that's bothering you. Kaho gave me a dagger once. I had just started working and I never could have paid him for it, but I can now. The man who sold you steel may have died, but Kaho is still alive, so I've got to settle my debt."

"You know that doesn't make any sense."

"If you don't want it, I won't ask for it."

"It's not right."

Go was confused about what exactly was "not right," most likely because Chigiri herself didn't really know what she wanted or what she planned to refuse. After several conversations, Go wondered if his idea was just out of line. Perhaps Chigiri accepted it because, while it was just talk, she preferred to get along, while a hard core in her rejected it outright.

More or less satisfied with this conclusion, he found himself busy with work and able to avoid thinking about her for a while. February and March were busy months in the television industry just prior to the new programming season. It was inconvenient for him to leave Tokyo.

After a time, Chigiri sent him a picture postcard.

Hakusan is still white with snow. I hear Tokyo has already had its first spring wind. I imagine you're having lots of fun all the time. Spring is still a while off here, but I'd love to take you to see the field of fawn lilies at Heisenji Temple.

That night he called Tsurugi.

"So, where is this Heisenji?"

"I can't believe a TV producer has never heard of such a famous temple. Do you know Echizen Katsuyama?"

"No, can't say I do."

"You're hopeless. What about Hakusan?"

"Give me some credit."

"It's to the south of Hakusan. Hakusan is between Tsurugi and Heisenji."

"And what sort of flowers are these fawn lilies?"

"They're quite nice."

Go was feeling vexed that the conversation wasn't getting to the point.

"So you'll take me there?"

"If you'd like to see them, Mr. Imai."

"No more 'Mr. Imai,' please."

"If you'd like to see them, Go."

"I would. When would be a good time?"

"The fawn lily usually blooms in April, but I don't know about this year. I'll call the tourism bureau at Katsuyama."

Go opened up his schedule and gave her three dates.

"Saturday is best for me," she put in.

"Why's that?"

"Mayu will be home to look after her grandfather."

And that settled the matter. Go didn't care whether or not the flowers were in bloom, and, for that matter, neither did Chigiri. But at least they had figured out how to get together again without the crucial subject hanging over them.

Heisenji, tucked into the mountains southeast of Katsuyama City, has a long history, and there are historical landmarks and famous places by the dozen in the area. There are some fawn lilies along the temple paths, but nobody ever goes there just to see them.

Rather than taking the train all the way to Kanazawa and then driving back to Tsurugi, to the top of Hakusan and down over the pass to Katsuyama and Heisenji Temple, it made much more sense for someone coming from Tokyo to change trains at Fukui and take a private line directly to Katsuyama.

Be that as it may, on the first Saturday of April, Go duly arrived at Kanazawa Station at about two, and he and Chigiri drove through the mountains, where the shadows of evening had already begun to fall, and on into the tunnel that took them from Kaga to Echizen, on their way to see the fawn lilies at Heisenji. Go left the driving to Chigiri. There were many things he wanted to say to her, but the mountain road had them so close to the edge that he could see straight down into the valley below. Chigiri, hands gripping the steering wheel, concentrated on her driving. Go didn't want to distract her with conversation, although unbeknownst to him, the tension she was feeling was not entirely the fault of the narrow road.

"That mountain is Dainichisan," said Chigiri, offering a word of explanation. "And there's a paulownia, but it's too early for flowers yet."

"I saw them back by Tedorigawa. The blooms were just opening."

"Are you sure?"

"I could be wrong."

"They're a light purple, like wisteria."

"You're named after the paulownia—it's quite an elegant name."

"I've never lived up to it."

"I couldn't say. I've never seen a thousand paulownia all at once."

"You're supposed to say, 'No, of course that's not true!'"

"It's not true."

"Too late. Go, you are not very good at flattering women."

"It depends on the woman."

"Is that so?"

"I can say anything to someone I don't care about. I don't mind being cocky, and it doesn't embarrass me."

"Heisenji used to have six thousand *bo*."

"What's a *bo*?"

"The temples have monks, right? I think the *bo* were the monks serving as the temple's private army."

"The thing is, when it comes to someone who's important to me, I can't say anything right. I sound like an asshole. I sound serious when I'm not, and when I want to be serious, I act like an idiot."

"Those six thousand *bo* were all killed in the Ikko Uprising."

"I told you I made love to a woman I had just met that day. But really, I didn't."

Chigiri laughed, and Go went on glumly.

"There're all kinds of things that mean nothing. But some things *are* important. Some things need to be spelled out."

"You mean that woman?"

"That woman meant nothing to me."

"So what do you mean by important things?"

"I want you to believe me when I tell you I never slept with her."

"All right then, I believe you."

"You're lying."

By that time they had arrived in Katsuyama. As they were passing through town, Chigiri spoke as if just remembering.

"Oh, have you decided where you're going to stay tonight?"

"Not yet."

"I've got a place I'd like to take you. It's an old house near Heisenji; it belongs to a *kocho* family."

"*Kocho*?"

"Landowners who built enormous homes, expensive mansions. They'd love to have someone in TV visit. I'm supposed to take you there on the way back from seeing the fawn lilies. I think they'd like you to stay overnight."

"I don't mind."

He tried to sound casual, but as soon as he spoke he smelled Chigiri's body next to his. He kept his face pointed straight ahead, but looked down at her knees and legs. He wanted to put his hand on her soft, round thighs, and he tried to keep himself from thinking there might be a chance to do so that night. He knew Chigiri might be planning to leave him there and drive back to Tsurugi alone, and he didn't know how he would comfort himself if he got his expectations up only to be disappointed.

"The homes of the rich around here are incredible. But I hear the families who own them live in Tokyo and hire people to keep the places up. My father's cousin is one of the hired hands. Her job is to rent out rooms for tea ceremonies, and invite historians and photographers to stay. Her name is Matsuko and she has been there for years. They trust her with everything."

"Sounds better than a tiny room in a business hotel."

"I said she was my father's cousin. Actually, she was the wife of my father's brother's son. The son, my cousin, found another woman and ran off to Kyoto, so she divorced him and started working at the mansion. She's getting up in years, but she's a great cook."

"So you've already told her we'd stop by."

"Well, we don't have to if you don't want to."

"No, contrary to appearances, I like ancient stuff, all that history stuff."

"There are two red pine trees in place of a front gate. It's a substantial lot, but it's like a haunted house because Matsuko rattles around inside all alone."

It was already five. It would be night by the time they had seen the flowers and stopped at the mansion. They could always head back to Kanazawa for the night, but he decided to go along with Chigiri's plan. He promised himself he wouldn't object even if she left him alone in Katsuyama.

The trip made him feel free and happy, but then his thoughts would return to the wad of bills he had packed in his bag. He was used to carrying money around to pay expenses when on a shoot, but it felt different this time, heavier.

Neither of them was sure of their ultimate destination. Was it the fawn lilies, the mansion with the red pines, or a hotel in Katsuyama or Kanazawa?

Chigiri had described the old home in the village of Heisenji as a haunted house. It was actually its garden that was worth seeing. It had a winding stream and artificial hills, and an old-fashioned warehouse that faced southeast, into the sun. It was the sort of garden historians and photographers loved. And, as with many of the grand old houses in the area, the homes were set up to receive overnight visitors. Just as Heisenji, surrounded by a forest of cedars hid its fortunes from the rest of the world, so did this home conceal the prosperity of its owners.

But, as with the fawn lilies, Chigiri and Go really didn't care about that. Compared to the currents of feeling between man and woman, neither history nor power held much interest.

Chigiri didn't want Go to know that she had told Mayu she might not be home that night, or that she had called the Kimura mansion and let the unflappable Matsuko know that she might be stopping by with a TV producer, and that he might be spending the night.

Matsuko had urged Chigiri, in her usual easygoing voice, to stay over herself. "You need a break from taking care of your father." Matsuko spoke frankly, and even commandingly, for a woman who had spent half of her life as a servant. Behind Chigiri's invitation to show Go the lilies was an unconscious desire to introduce him to Matsuko.

They arrived at Heisenji, got out of the car, and slowly climbed the road up to the main temple, unhampered by other visitors, but they turned back partway when it got too cold to go on. The cedar forest surrounding the temple was so dense, and the trees so large and ancient, that they expected to see ghosts or evil spirits come flying out at any moment. When the tension and anxiety she had brought along was compounded with this, Chigiri became so frightened that she asked Go if they could return the way they had come.

"These cedars are too tall and forbidding for their own good," he agreed.

"Yes, they're not as twisted and cynical as the Rokuro Cedar. I like trees that are a little less sure of themselves. These look like they might go after little girls."

"Cedars are bold trees; they are rarely ignored or abused."

"They grow so straight."

"And quickly, so the wood can be used for lumber."

"They're lucky, but that's why I hate them. They're always looking down on those of us who are less fortunate. Pine can be used to make charcoal, but cedars are only useful for building big houses."

"But some are like the Rokuro Cedar."

"That one I like. It lets you sit on its branches. And nobody knows about it—even in Tsurugi."

Chigiri had a purple shawl with a blue border wrapped around her shoulders instead of a coat. The tips of her fingers had gone white gripping it close for warmth. Her hair had grown some since Go had last seen her, and she had pulled the waves together, tying them up softly at the nape of her neck. The stray hairs at her ears and over her forehead seemed to reduce her age to that of a schoolgirl, but her cheeks were taut and the tip of her nose red. Go thought she looked like she was in her mid-thirties. She had the worldly burdens of divorce, poverty and an invalid father, but he was sure that it was her gentle disposition and lack of practicality that kept her so young.

Chigiri, too, was studying Go. For a man of forty-seven, his stomach was flat, and he didn't have extra weight on his back or shoulders either, but his eyes and his cheeks drooped, and he had a lot of gray in his hair.

But he doesn't come across as old; it must be because he's bashful. Not the shyness of a boy. Over and over he's run into situations he couldn't resolve, try as he might, and tasted failure again and again. Yet somehow he couldn't stop hoping, and he feels a sort of pity, a sense of humor about the way he is. An involuted, rogueish bashfulness. My liking it—makes me a rogue too.

She mentally squared her shoulders as she thought, *Rogue.*

"The flowers are this way."

Leaving the car on the shoulder of the road, Chigiri led the way. The sun in the Western sky was bright. Chigiri walked on with an ear to the sound of Go's footsteps right behind her. Go kept up, careful to stay in the comfort of her shadow, which fell on the lower part of his body and felt good. Its movement over his back and thighs sent a thrill through him.

Part of the road to Heisenji was overgrown with the dark, vast forest of cedars, but there was a treeless hill close by that was covered in the deep purple of the fawn lilies. At the tips of stalks rising from among the soft leaves were small blossoms that resembled the cyclamen. The purple flames flickered in the breeze.

Even though fawn lilies grow in profusion, they are not a ground cover. A close look revealed weeds and other plants in the wet ground. But with the flowers all standing in bloom, the entire slope was dyed in their color. Crouching down for a better look revealed an even darker purple and the appearance of an undulating wave.

Chigiri stood in the middle of the road and looked down at the hill.

"See? There they are," she spoke with pride. "This is the best view."

When Go came up and stood next to her, he saw that the hill spread out to his left, and, he discovered that to his right, a triangular patch of land surrounded by a border of trees was also in bloom.

"What a sight. I wish I had my camera."

"A woman reporter would probably gush for you: 'Oh! It's just so beautiful!'"

"I'd like to do away with that. Beautiful, delicious, wonderful. I need to find a reporter who won't use any of those words."

"Why don't you just tell them to say something else?"

"They'd be speechless. There are lots of girls like that. The leaves and the flowers look so soft."

"They taste good, too."

"You eat them?"

"In salads and sandwiches."

"Sounds more and more like a topic for a TV show."

"It's not the sort of flavor a reporter would get all excited about. It's bitter, but good. Matsuko might fix some for us tonight."

Go picked a flower at his feet, and nibbled at a petal. It was not so bitter as sweet, almost like the flavor of a woman's cologne.

"So, how does it taste?"

"It's not bitter."

With a mischievous glint in her eye, Chigiri plucked Go's finger, flower and all, and brought it up to her face and bit the petal at the same spot he had. When she let go of his hand, all that was left in it was a little bit of petal.

It was the first time they had touched. When she'd left him at the station the time before, they hadn't shaken hands. They hadn't even brushed against each other this time, on the drive from Kanazawa to Heisenji.

Chigiri had pulled his finger to her mouth so quickly and unexpectedly that neither of them felt the warmth of each other until it was all over. While Chigiri chewed on the flower petal, almost like a child, the softness of her hand flooded Go's senses. Chigiri felt like she was munching on Go himself, and not just on the petal he had tasted first.

"Doesn't it taste like a cosmetic, maybe a fragrance?" Go spoke to Chigiri's plump, moving lips.

"No."

"That's what it tasted like to me."

"I've never had any fragrance that smelled like this."

Go felt like Chigiri was scolding him. And even that sent waves of longing flooding through him.

"There's probably a particular woman you're thinking of."

"No, I don't think so."

"It's got to be. Fragrance doesn't taste this green."

Go was enraptured with her. Her strength and something deep in those beguiling eyes had burst open. It was small and sad and desperate enough to shut him up.

"Well, who knows?"

"I'm telling you, it's not a fragrance, it's the smell of some woman."

Go was quiet as he did everything in his power to keep his impulses under control. Chigiri misunderstood that silence.

"See? Now you've remembered who it was."

"No."

"Oh, it doesn't matter." The wind had gotten stronger, and Chigiri's fingers gripped her shawl. "Why didn't you leave that bag in the car?"

The bag wasn't large, and Go walked with the strap over his shoulder. It contained clean underwear, his shaving kit, and cash.

"There's money, so I don't like to leave it anywhere." It was a relief to finally mention it, and he quickly added, "It's the way I've always carried my money with me. You'd be surprised how much I have when I go out on long shoots. I wear shabby-looking clothes and dirty sneakers, and carry this bag with me everywhere I go. In some of the countries I've been, inflation is so bad, I have to keep it packed with bills. But I've never been robbed."

The truth was that he was eager to be rid of its contents. He wanted all of the money out before the trip back to Tokyo, and just mentioning that he had it made him feel more relaxed.

"So, shall we go to the Kimura mansion, then?" he suggested. "I'd be delighted to eat something made from these flowers."

This time Go led the way. He could hear Chigiri's steps, less steady now, but he didn't care. He'd mentioned the money, so he could walk on straight ahead. He went quickly down the road that divided the swath of purple in two, back to where the car was parked.

He was afraid that if he turned around to look at her, he'd be shy and hesitant all over again.

5

LATER, WHEN GO IMAI LOOKED back on that day, the first thing he remembered was the field of fawn lilies. Right in the middle of it there was a patch of white light. He ran straight into the light, and there he found a—what was it? It was a hole that felt like a soft, marshy wetland. But that didn't mean it felt good. No, it was suffocating.

He wasn't sure where that image came from, but it was always the way his memories of the day began. From there he would crawl out of the white light in the midst of the flowers, and head for the Kimura mansion, and, by and by, Chigiri would be walking next to him.

The bookmark for that memory was always on the page where the fawn lilies appeared. There was more written on that page than he was aware of, and the content was much more complicated than he could have imagined. In the end, he was never sure whether it had been a good day or a bad one.

As for Chigiri, every time she remembered the day, she was embarrassed and dumbfounded at her own actions. It was as if she was unable to recognize herself throughout the events that began that morning and continued late into the night.

Matsuko was waiting for the two when they arrived at the Kimura home. Go remembered her as wearing a kimono, while Chigiri would later insist that it had been a sweater and skirt. They were both wrong. Matsuko had gone out during the afternoon to buy fish that had been caught that morning, and she was still wearing her work clothes that evening.

This just went to prove that the more seriously they considered the matter, the more their versions varied because they had both been focused so intently on different things. It was one miscalculation and misunderstanding after another, and the greatest of these was about where they were going to spend the night. Go, of course, hoped it would be the Kimura mansion where they were headed. He was clueless, however, as to whether Chigiri was planning to stay with him, and unable to ask her. He had some vague notion of handing over the money that hurt like a pair of too-small shoes, and wordlessly sending her on her way. Chigiri, for her part, had gone over and over the scenario for the evening, and knew every gesture and line by heart. By the time she had picked him up that afternoon, she was finally able to walk and breathe naturally, but it hadn't been easy. What she hadn't counted on was the inability of men to understand the depth of a woman's resolution. It is why men appear timid and nervous at critical moments when women appear so clearly in control. Women are determined and tenacious when men are of precious little use merely because women lack adaptability; it is impossible for them to take a step or speak a word unless they have thought things over thoroughly and adopted a plan of action.

"These must be the gatepost pines," Go said.

"That's right. They're pretty spindly, but that just adds to the air of a haunted house, don't you think?"

Go looked at Chigiri wondering why she so wanted him to believe it was an eerie place. The building in front of them was black and antiquated-looking, but it was obviously well kept up. The garden that spread out to their left was so neat as to be almost aloof. But on the opposite side was a young cherry in bloom.

"When you said haunted house, I imagined a deserted shack, but someone has put a lot of money into this."

"Did you know the camellia, cherry, forsythia and narcissus all bloom at the same time?"

"You don't mean just this house, do you?"

"No, this whole area. It's because the winters are long and cold. Spring comes all at once. Everything goes crazy—it's like they've got to bloom right now or they'll lose their chance."

They could see red flowers in the valley made by the artificial hills. *Those must be the camellia*, Go thought. The narcissus were at the side of the stream, while the forsythia bloomed among rocks to its side, little yellow flowers peeking out. Just as Chigiri had described it, it looked to Go as if they'd all gone mad jumping at their chance to make a splash. The sun was almost gone, and the scene was covered in a soft smoky-gray wash.

Suppressing a sense of urgency, Go followed Chigiri as she opened the door. From the smell of the cold, earthy house came the scent of wild camellia which had been tossed into a vase in the entryway; there were new buds on the branches.

"Matsuko!" Chigiri called out in a cheerful voice.

From far down the passageway the floorboards began to resound with the sound of light, quick steps.

"I've been waiting for you!" Matsuko quickly went down onto her knees in a formal greeting to Go, and it was too dark for him to see her face.

"I know this was sudden," he began.

"Of course it's not! Chigiri told me you would be here. I've seen your documentary, you know."

"I was just an assistant then."

"So were the fawn lilies in bloom?" Matsuko asked Chigiri.

"About halfway. Do you mean you don't know? I was looking forward to that dish you make with them."

"Oh it's made. We've got them in the garden."

Matsuko led them into a large room that was separated from the room next to it with sliding doors, but it was fully twelve mats. In one corner were the *tokonoma* alcove and a set of alcove shelves. The ceiling had been fitted with boards that had been painted, albeit long ago, with flowers of the season. The *tokonoma* housed a painting of a single pine tree on washi paper that took up the entire wall. Having been hung directly on the clay wall, it was spattered with water stains. An inkstone and brush had been placed on the alcove shelves, and Matsuko brought them over to Go along with a guestbook and placed them on a low table.

"I'll bring you tea. In the meantime, please sign the guestbook."

Go nodded in assent while grimacing at the brush. As soon as Matsuko left, he stood up and went over to the window. That section of the room had a wooden floor rather than tatami, and it was equipped with an *irori*, a sunken hearth, in the middle of it with charcoal already burning. The paper doors covering the windows were opened a crack, and he peeked out at the garden. He could see only a short distance as it was bathed in the purple-black of early nightfall; it was only visible as far as the light of the room could reach; a few forsythia among the rocks.

"Come now and write your name," Chigiri urged him. "It's proof that you've actually been here."

"Proof."

"She shows it to the owner when he comes down from Tokyo."

Left to themselves and prodded by Chigiri, Go didn't have a choice. He sat down at the table and opened the book. He noticed the name of a poet whose name he occasionally read in the newspaper. Next to his name was a little verse he had presumably composed for the occasion.

> The hearth is crackling,
> "How about a sip for me,
> of that clear sake?"

Someone had drawn a picture on the next page. A manga artist. He recognized the names of some photographers, and a professor from Tokyo had scribbled something in French.

"I don't have any tricks to show off. TV producers spend all their time getting other people to do their tricks." He sat there with the brush in his hand for a few moments before he resolutely wrote out his name and address.

"Don't forget the date."

"Of course."

"Why don't you attach your card?"

Go did as he was instructed. This way the owner would know for sure that someone in TV had been there. He sighed and thought guiltily of the bag of money in the corner of the room.

Matsuko came back with the tea and asked to confirm if Go would be staying the night.

"And you, too, Chigiri?"

Chigiri hesitated as if she were thinking the matter over, and finally indicated that she would. Go listened to this interchange, keeping his eye on the flames in the hearth.

Dinner was as delicious as Chigiri had hoped and much more so than anything Go had imagined. The cook obviously knew that city folk were used to the most tender of beef and expensive imported ingredients, and had taken a completely different tack.

The lightly broiled venison flavored in local miso smelled delicious. The fish Matsuko had bought that morning was not often seen in Tokyo, and the meat was thick and firm. There were dishes made using bamboo shoots and clams, with seeds from local trees added for a tantalizing aroma. She had prepared *chawanmushi* custard with steamed white fish and plum, and spread a bamboo leaf underneath to herald the season. Go had eaten some of these local specialties before in Kanazawa, but none had tasted as good. He finally recognized the fawn lilies mixed in with a bit of tofu in a bowl with a few other ingredients.

"I could have sworn these flowers tasted like cologne, but in this they are sweet."

"It's got both the leaves and the flowers in it," explained Matsuko as she filled his cup with hot sake, and Go looked again to see the pinkish color. "Rape blossoms and chrysanthemums are all sweet, but they're bitter, too. Flowers are sweet and bitter." Matsuko continued to talk as she set trout on the *irori* to cook.

Chigiri was entranced with the way Matsuko moved about taking care of things, and almost forgot to keep an eye on Go's cup of sake. She moved to pick up the bottle, but Go got to it first and held it out for her. Chigiri had no choice but to pick up her own cup to be filled.

"You're really not supposed to eat flowers," she noted.

"Why's that?"

"Plants put out their fruit after the flowers have bloomed. The fruit is what humans and other animals eat. It's against the rules to eat the flowers before they've had a chance to produce fruit. That's why they taste bitter. Isn't that right, Matsuko?"

Chigiri's voice sounded almost contentious, and Matsuko turned around to look at the pair, while her hands continued the work of adjusting the angle of the trout on skewers in front of her.

By the time Go and Chigiri had polished off the trout dipped in vinegar sauce and the buckwheat and Turkish delight dessert, they were thoroughly sated, and both slightly tipsy.

"How about some brown tea?" suggested Matsuko.

"I'd rather have something more stringent," said Go. Stronger tea should clear his head, he thought.

"I'll make it," said Chigiri and she stood up and left the room. Go and Matsuko were left alone together.

"I'm moved. What a delicious meal," sighed Go.

Matsuko's mouth bent in the very slightest of smiles.

"Mr. Imai, it wasn't my cooking that impressed you. It was this old house, this region, and Chigiri—she's much stronger than she looks, just so you know."

The mention of Chigiri's name threw Go off, and he wondered what Matsuko was trying to tell him.

"I know her father, Kaho, well, and I assume she takes after him," he assured her.

"Women can be stronger than men when they need to be."

Go had the idea that Matsuko realized something was up, but was letting him get away with it. He realized that he might be reading too much into it just because he felt guilty about the money, but at any rate—Matsuko's kindness set him on edge.

Chigiri made some strong green tea, put it on a tray and brought it in. Matsuko made a move to leave as soon as she arrived, but Chigiri stopped her. She wanted her to stay a little longer before she left her alone with Go.

"I called home, and Mayu told me she's made rice gruel for Dad and was just feeding him."

"I told you you should take some time off. Mayu's capable of more than you give her credit for. As for your father, he probably can't tell the two of you apart anymore. You're the one that always has to do things right; you've got to give yourself a break once in a while."

"I'm always giving myself a break. I haven't paid you back the money you lent us, have I?"

"That's exactly what I mean. You mention that loan every time I see you. I'll remember it without you having to remind me, so you can forget about it for a while. Isn't that the way things are, Mr. Imai? She's got it all backwards."

"I'm as stubborn as my father."

"You've got to depend on others to take care of things once in a while."

"Matsuko is always complaining about me." Chigiri sounded almost sulky, and her face turned pink as she spoke to Go, but he could only laugh. He didn't want to get involved in family matters. He understood that both Chigiri and Matsuko were treating him with a great deal of familiarity, but he wasn't sure just how close they would allow him to get.

"I think I'll have something to eat in the kitchen," said Matsuko. "The bath is ready, and I've laid out Mr. Imai's bedding upstairs. Chigiri, I think you can take care of your own. If you need anything, Mr. Imai, have Chigiri take care of it for you. You can leave the charcoal—I'll put it out later."

Upstairs there were two rooms divided by sliding paper doors, one larger than the other. The larger one was similar to the one downstairs. The low table had been moved to the side, and Go's bedding had been laid out in the middle.

Chigiri led Go upstairs and, just like a hotel maid might, she efficiently and rather distantly told him where he could find his sleeping yukata, jacket, towel and toothbrush, and told him to help himself to the bath. He dutifully headed off back downstairs. The bathroom was dark, and after he had soaked for a while in the tub, he went back up to his room. Chigiri was gone. He opened the sliding doors ever so slightly and got a glimpse of the bedding she had laid out for herself and her purple shawl with the blue border tossed on top.

After about twenty minutes she came up the stairs with a pitcher of ice water.

"I brought some water, or would beer have been better?"

"No, I don't need any more liquor. Look, let's get this over with. I want to give it to you before I forget." He pulled the wad of bills wrapped in paper out of his bag and put it on the table. His gesture was clinical, almost as if he'd taken out a souvenir from Tokyo he'd brought along.

"Thank you very much," Chigiri bowed her head, but her face was expressionless. She couldn't bring herself to touch the money, so Go reached over and set it on her lap.

"I'm sorry for all the trouble."

"Please don't apologize."

"You're right."

"It's a relief to be done with it." Go wanted to laugh it off, but the tension Chigiri reeked of had infected him, too. He had felt the warmth of her thighs when he set the money on her lap, but he couldn't bring himself to reach over and touch them again. "Why don't you put that away somewhere."

"Of course." Chigiri snapped to attention, and disappeared into the next room. Go heard her go downstairs, and when she returned after a while, she was wearing a yukata that matched his. Her hair was down, and her skin was pale for someone who had just stepped out of a hot bath. The only clue was a touch of perspiration on her nose. She turned down the comforter on the bedding, and sat waiting for Go to make his move. As determined as she appeared, Go also got the feeling that she was defeated, and he himself was at an utter loss.

"This is my end of the deal," she said. The clarity of her voice contrasted so greatly with the confusion Go felt that he was almost angry. He went over to her side, and almost pushed her down on her back.

"Now what do I do? What do you want me to do?" he growled.

"I'm the one that's supposed to be asking that."

"If you don't want me here, I'll leave."

"You can't. We've decided to do it like this."

Go, to his amazement, found all other paths closed to him. He didn't have a choice, he thought, as he climbed on top of her. He brushed his lips against hers, but not knowing if it was what she wanted, he quickly drew back. Chigiri's eyes were closed with her face leaning ever so slightly to the right. A drop of perspiration sparkled near her left eye.

He could feel her body heat and her quickening pulse through the yukata. Go sighed. But that was his upper body. His organ was hard and large enough for Chigiri to feel. He opened the front of his yukata and it was like an animal that had been kept in check and now set free. Chigiri shifted her legs as if they too were uncomfortable and eager to move.

She was naked under her yukata, and Go felt her pubic hair on his stomach. He wanted only to escape, and to that end he penetrated her. Chigiri's face went red, but the expression on her face, still tilted to one side, was unchanged, her beautiful lips were closed. Her yukata was neatly crossed at her breast. He was distressed that he had moved so quickly without a kiss or caress, and now he was deep inside her.

The feeling that he needed to start all over again, to go back to the beginning, seeped up in his heart like an underwater stream, but he was terrified to let go of her. He wouldn't know what to do then. He finally decided he'd have to run for the finish line.

He stopped looking at her face. He knew her expression had changed but couldn't say whether it was in agony or in pleasure, and he was afraid of how he would feel if he knew which it was. The more beautiful she was, the more he hated himself. Go repeated the motions he knew would get him through to ejaculation. If he could climb up *there*, everything else would sort itself out.

Sweat dripped from under his yukata. He made it to the top of the zigzag staircase that reached to the sky, then writhed further up a spiral staircase. Then started running again, taking an occasional breather. But then he'd wonder what it was he thought he was doing to this woman before realizing he couldn't worry about that now, and started moving again.

He'd be empty before long. He leaped towards that emptiness. He could see it shining before him, but couldn't quite reach it. There was something in the way.

He continued to move blindly; all thought of how it felt to him was gone. He simply beat his organ against the dead-end it encountered.

Just then, Chigiri's head thrust upward and moved back and forth. Her breathing was ragged as she gave out a cry. At that instant the soft flesh enveloping the part of him inside her convulsed.

Go was alarmed at what was happening beneath him, and he stopped. Her voice was tapering off and her head was still in motion. He saw tears at the corners of her tightly closed eyes.

Go reflexively held her head to his chest, as one might do to protect a weaker thing. He held his breath and waited. The muscles holding him so tightly inside her relaxed, and her body went quiet.

It was Go who finally groaned "Ahhh," not out of ecstasy, but because his heart was pounding so hard. Chigiri's intense release had gone not below his waist, but to the center of his being. His erection had subsided without a release, but he was still inside of her. And he didn't feel he could move now that she had reached her climax.

"I'm so sorry," Chigiri apologized with her head turned to the side.

"Why are you apologizing?"

"It's been two years since…"

"And?"

"It wasn't part of the bargain," she groaned, and then started as she came to a new realization. "Was it just me?"

"That's all right."

"No, it's not all right. What should I do?"

Chigiri tried to hold him inside of her at the very instant he withdrew.

"No! I can't leave it there."

Chigiri wrapped her face in her hands and tried to hide under the comforter, and then she began to cry. Her hair was stuck to her neck, and her bright red earlobe was like a flower on top of it.

Go couldn't understand why Chigiri, who had been so businesslike a few minutes before, was now so distraught, but it made him even fonder of her. He didn't know what to do about her insistence that it was not right. He gently pulled the wet hairs off her neck.

"What's the matter?"

"I was the only one who got it."

"Huh?"

Her face was pressed into the bedding, so he couldn't hear her too well, but the very word sounded new to him. He understood it, of course. Such a common word, oft-used…and suddenly he felt as if he had been pulled into her past.

"I'm not as young as I used to be; these things happen sometimes. But I'm fine with it."

The loss of youth had nothing to do with it, this was more psychological. If it were a one-off, a woman he had paid for a single act, he would have gotten right down to business and been done with it, so age was not a factor.

"I got the feeling and I didn't do anything for you."

"Was that what you said before? 'Got'?"

Chigiri was silent, but the red of her earlobe had spread to her neck. Go finally peeled the comforter away from her face, pulled her back to him, and buried his lips in hers. As his tongue moved, he wondered if she'd had so much experience "getting it" that using that verb had become natural to her. Yet, at the same time, she didn't understand anything about him. The thought was vexing.

"I haven't given you anything…in return."

She barely managed to get the words out, Go had her so tightly confined. The scenario she had gone over and over in her mind had been completely abandoned by her body, and she was annoyed. It was as though she had doubled her debt. On top of that, the area below her belly was still churning. She couldn't even think of how she would repay him until she was back in control of herself.

"Wait, please…just a little while."

She didn't look him in the eye, and without knowing what it was she wanted to wait for, he agreed. Then they both closed their eyes as if to clear their minds. Go's organ conveniently settled down, and Chigiri fell into a light sleep. She opened her eyes and met Go's. For minutes now he had been watching Chigiri's face. It was clean of all make-up, and he was thinking about how beautiful she was. He examined her features and concluded the sensual impression came from her thick eyebrows, her slightly plump eyelids, and the vertical lines in her full lips.

All Chigiri could think of was her powerlessness, how embarrassed she felt and her need to rectify this impossible situation. Making up her mind, she untied the sash on her yukata and reached out for Go's. With both of them naked, the ceiling seemed much higher and the room larger. Unwrapped and revealed, her body felt small and useless. Go wrapped his arms around her shoulders, and Chigiri embraced his waist, and they could not do otherwise.

"I'd made my decision," said Chigiri.

Go looked puzzled. "Yes?"

"I'm going to be your prostitute."

Go laughed out loud, but stopped suddenly. "Chigiri, everything you do is a surprise. You sounded cheery and pleasant when you said you were poor. Nobody uses the word 'prostitute' these days, it almost makes me feel nostalgic."

"Well, it's the only word I know."

"You think you become a prostitute just by accepting money? Well, you can't."

"It's better that way. I can."

Looking into her eyes, Go could not laugh. Instead, his lips drew closer to her and were soon all over hers, her tongue, her neck, her chin. Chigiri tried to shake them off as she began to lick Go's chest, then his stomach, and finally the part below—where she came face to face with his earnest erection.

"Make it smaller."

"Why?"

"I'm going to do this from the beginning."

"You're breathing on it; it's impossible."

But now Go knew what Chigiri meant by "prostitute." He had to stifle a laugh, but it had the effect she demanded. Then a little more. Now he was relaxed. He wasn't old yet, but he wasn't young either.

Chigiri's lips touched it gingerly. The deflated organ reassured her somewhat, and she grew more bold. As soon as she had it in her mouth, a thrill shot threw Go's body.

Grabbing her hair he said, "Not a prostitute, okay?"

Chigiri was unable to respond. Her lips and tongue were not working to speak; they were volunteering for the sake of an organ that could respond to the tiniest variation of pressure or force.

Go's repressed groans encouraged her, and she felt as if she was doing something good. She was giving Go pleasure, and this gave her energy and fueled her own desire, and she forgot what she had planned to do next. She was flustered the instant her mouth was empty again.

She felt her body being lifted, as Go pulled her up. She couldn't see his expression because the light was behind him, but the light in his eyes shone through.

"My sweet little prostitute."

"Yes?"

"Are you mine? This too? And this?"

"Yes."

"Can I make sure?"

"Of course."

Go's tongue didn't wait for Chigiri's response to begin sucking her nipples. Chigiri held her voice. Her head whipped back and forth again. His tongue moved down to her navel and then straight down from there. It arrived at the place Chigiri was afraid it might.

She had thought through this evening over and over and over again, mulling the details she was determined to see through. But the instant she had imagined Go's lips on a certain part of her body, she had lost her grip and all her confidence. And there he was now, just as she was congratulating herself on accomplishing her own goal.

Exceeding Chigiri's expectations, all of her mental rehearsal and resolve built thereupon, Go's tongue instantly shot an electric wave through flesh that was as lively as a little fish, and through the small moist window within it, numbing every inch of her body.

When the current ran from her nether regions to her stomach, up to her throat and out her mouth, Go's tongue picked up its pace in an effort to make that voice louder and stronger.

Chigiri was defeated, but was not quite ready to give up. She wanted more. The instant she spoke up to ask for it, she achieved an ecstasy equal to the ferocity of her defeat.

"You want more?"

"Yes. More than before," she pleaded looking into his eyes.

Go penetrated Chigiri, aiming for the height he hadn't quite achieved the first time. He kept his mouth on hers to keep her quiet, but their voices went back and forth down each other's throats, expanding, then breaking, scattering. Covered in sparks, assailed by a sensation akin to unbearable pain, the two were tossed out of the world.

Chigiri's mind and body continued to reverberate with the pleasure, and she repeated to herself the excuse that it had been two years since she had had this. *That's why. That's.* She finally began to cry. Go bit his lip to avoid saying what he felt. *You're no prostitute. You could never be one.*

They were still physically linked together, but thinking separate thoughts. That is the way it is with most men and women, and Go and Chigiri were no exception. They touched each other's shoulders and backs with their nose and fingertips, snuggling close. A vague fear kept either of them from uttering the words that welled up in them.

6

In 1978, A DAM WAS built upstream on the Tedorigawa, putting an end to the floods that had plagued Tsurugi since recorded history. This was three years before Go Imai and Chigiri Yamazaki met up again after twenty-five years. An elementary school and middle school were built in 1980, and a village partway up Hakusan completed a municipal gymnasium. During those years, there was always something new for the folks in Tsurugi to see and talk about. Japan's economic growth made the faintest of headways even into the backwaters of the Hokuriku region. Eventually, however, the thrill wore off, and everyone went back to his or her usual, unexciting way of life. By then, only a few were able to reflect on and appreciate the fact that the town was no longer prone to regular flooding. There were very few people who were still frightened by the prospect of a deluge, most likely because almost twenty years had passed since Tedorigawa had reached a level of 280 centimeters; it had been in 1961 during the deadly Second Muroto Typhoon when the town had last put emergency measures into action to save it from flooding.

Kaho had a clear memory of that brush with disaster, and it seemed to grow more vivid the more demented he became. Whenever they had a long rain, he never failed to start calling out to Chigiri to take up the tatami and keep it dry. Chigiri always laughed and told him they had the dam to protect them now, but that didn't help. What would happen to them if the dam broke, he moaned, his eyes rolling in agitation. Then when the weather improved, he'd start demanding that she do something to get ready for the next storm. He'd toss a box of tissue paper at her to get her attention. She'd finally have to tell him she was on her way to city hall to talk to someone about the matter, and then she'd go outside to weed for a while until he forgot about the river. Once she was back inside he might launch into a lecture on the route Toshiie Maeda took to invade Kaga, sending Chigiri to the kitchen for refuge. From there all she had to do was call out "I see" or "you don't say" occasionally to keep him satisfied.

The spring and summer of 1981 were unseasonably cold in Tsurugi. Some of the good citizens were sincerely concerned that it was because Tedorigawa had been dammed upstream, but for Chigiri it was an unsettling period that left her entirely numb. Not only had Kaho become so senile that he had begun abusing her, turning violent, but, and this was of even greater concern, Go Imai was continuing to cast fire into her life.

She had the ability to improve her situation and that of her family using the money Go had given her, and the time was coming when she would have no other choice but to do so. Yet, Chigiri was terrified of touching the money. Part of the problem was the odd notion that once she spent all the money, Go and her "prostitute" self would be gone forever.

Neither Go nor Chigiri made an attempt to contact the other for a couple of weeks after their stay at the Kimura mansion. Go came back to Kanazawa a little more than a month later, in mid-May. A friend of his was in the Kanazawa National Hospital, and he had come to see him. Go and Chigiri met at a hotel for a late lunch, and then he hurried off before visiting hours were over. He had business the next morning in Kyoto and he couldn't stay. Chigiri was hurt that it was all so rushed, but she was also irritated at herself for feeling that way. As they waited outside the hotel for an empty taxi, Chigiri thanked Go for the umpteenth time that day. *The money has been such a great help!* Each time she said it, Go had responded that he was glad to know that.

When an empty taxi arrived, they smiled uncomfortably at each other as they waved good-bye. Chigiri was unable to admit that she hadn't spent a single yen of that money. Go hadn't asked her how she had spent it, and, indeed, had avoided the subject altogether. Nor had he asked about Kaho and how he was doing. He didn't bring up their stay at the Kimura mansion. All he talked about was the friend he was planning to see that afternoon. He talked about the man, a friend who had looked after him when he was young. The friend was single and past seventy and had spent his life writing poems. And now he had an incurable disease.

The man was a shirttail relative, there was no blood connection, and Go had always wondered if he had stayed single because he had fallen in love with Go's mother as a youth. Chigiri commented on how romantic that sounded, and to think, the man was right here in Kanazawa.

"No," Go responded, "he lives in Maibara, but his doctor sent him to the hospital here."

"Is that so?"

"It's the truth."

"Has he been hospitalized long?"

"No, he came because he was told he didn't have long to live."

And that was the end of the conversation. Go hadn't lied about everything, but the man of whom he spoke had died several years before in Maibara. Go had the taxi driver drive him halfway around the city to go see a man who was long dead. He slunk down in the seat, sick with disappointment that he hadn't read what he'd been looking for in Chigiri's expression, and disgusted with himself for not being able to let her know what it was he had so hoped for.

On the train to Kyoto, Go thought about how Chigiri had claimed that the money he had given her had been of such help. He had searched desperately, but her expression had said nothing more to him than exactly that. He was disappointed, but decided that it was all just as well. On the other hand, he could just as well have reserved a room in a hotel and made love to her that afternoon. It would have made everything so much neater, and Chigiri might have preferred it that way, too. Not to mention it was what he had intended to do and why he had come to Kanazawa.

He had wanted her to show him that she had come for the same reason and that she wanted it as much as he did. Go wanted to see his simple needs reflected in Chigiri. He hadn't called her for two weeks because he was afraid that if he told her he wanted to see her while the money was still fresh on her mind, she might agree just because she felt she owed it to him, and he didn't want her to think that was what he was looking for. If Chigiri contacted him or otherwise indicated that she wanted to see him it would have been different.

Go had found a reason to go to Kyoto just so he could see her, and the first thing she did was thank him for the money. She said it had been a great help. Somehow it didn't please him at all, and he couldn't bring himself to tell her how much he wanted to hold her. Instead he said: as soon as he'd paid his friend a visit he had to go to Kyoto. It never occurred to him how much those words had hurt her.

His words, however, gave Chigiri an opportunity to make some changes. She finally decided she could use the money. Hadn't she told him she already had, and hadn't he approved? One of Mayu's schoolmates' father was a surgeon with his own practice, and she went to talk to him. She was treading on the toes of the doctor her father had been seeing for years, but she finally managed to have Kaho admitted into the Tsurugi Municipal Hospital. Kaho had begun waking her up at night complaining that he couldn't breathe. The more he struggled, the more difficult his breathing, and Chigiri had been at wit's end watching him.

Not only did she have to pay the hospital fees, but she had to hire someone to attend to him. He had objected to a room with five other patients, so she paid extra to move him to a room for two. But if something happened at night a nurse would be there, and during the day Chigiri had only to take her turn caring for him. A few days after Kaho had settled in, she found a part-time job at a sushi shop that was a five-minute walk from the hospital.

Four evenings a week, from five to nine, she carried orders up to the customers on the second floor of the shop and cleaned up after they left. The owner was an old friend of Matsuko's, and he was the second-generation owner of a cooking knife that Kaho had made. He didn't overwork Chigiri, so her main concern was watching the steps as she went up and down with trays of food and empty dishes. It was her first break from caring for her father since her divorce and she decided that she had to thank Go for making it possible.

He's either dissatisfied with my body, or he's doing lots of other things that are more fun. Chigiri imagined what Go's life was like. She decided that she would offer him her body if he asked, and act like there was nothing between them if he didn't. At least that was what she told herself when she found herself feeling doubtful. He had come all the way to Kanazawa to have lunch with her without showing the slightest interest in making love to her again. Maybe the word "prostitute" had put him off, she thought, regretting that she had used it.

She had grown used to Kaho waking her up in the middle of the night, coughing or pounding on the tatami to get her attention. Now all that was gone, and what she gained since the night became more private for her was a deeper sleep, thanks partly to working in the evening, and a greater awareness of her sexual appetite. The trickiest time came in the darkness of her room before she fell asleep, when she ruminated over what had happened at the Kimura mansion.

Was it like this? No, it must have been about here, she thought to herself as she used her fingers to check the spots. The darkness worked a magic charm on her. It turned into a long tongue that penetrated her body. She was drawn into its pleasure, but it was completely different from what had happened to her at the Kimura mansion. When she tried to make out Go's face in the black space, her heightened sensations quickly dissipated. She wasn't sure why, but had the feeling that if she wanted a re-enactment of what had happened, she would have to have Go's body pressed against hers. She quickly dismissed his face and the pleasure of her own actions returned.

Groaning in a voice too low for Mayu, on the second floor, to hear, and covered in sweat, she brought Go's face back and surprised herself. Even though she'd gotten rid of him, his face was dripping in sweat, too, and he gasped for air, his organ still inside her. It was as if he had been with her through the churning. She felt satisfied but also not, and irritated, and while still perplexed fell asleep. Not even then did she examine how she felt about Go. She'd been paid, so what would be the point? When she thought of his face, it wasn't the pleasure of sex that welled up within her but something else that included a psychological complex hidden away somewhere in her body. But even that complex was sexual in the end, so it made no sense to her. It was best not to think about it at all.

The matter of where a woman's emotions for a man are located is complicated, and there is no simple answer. In Chigiri's case, the feelings were a tangle of strings running through her body that were being tugged on and spun out, with an unmistakably sexual influence on her. It made her look younger and more beautiful.

"So, Mom, it turns out we had money after all."

This was what Mayu had to say when she learned her grandfather would be going to the hospital. She was the person closest to Chigiri, and the change apparent in her mother made her feel lonely. It was the instinctive reaction of a young girl to the beauty newly exuding from her mother.

Chigiri kept her back turned on her daughter as she responded.

"Money? Of course we don't have any. That's why I'm looking for a job."

The tone of Chigiri's voice notified Mayu that the conversation was over, and Mayu decided not to ask about the occasional late-night phone calls. The conversations were not particularly long and didn't sound urgent, but the way her mother ran to pick up the phone as soon as it began to ring tugged at her intuition. Could it have been an emergency at the sushi shop? Or from the hospital? She was alert to the situation, but her imagination couldn't take her very far for details.

Three men sat in office chairs and on the sofa by the window of Century Union Go on the sixth floor of the Akasaka building. They were watching the editing monitor, which was showing *Man of Aran*, a British film by Robert J. Flaherty, the father of the documentary. The sound had been turned off and the black-and-white film was scratchy, so the effects of the wind and waves made greater impressions than the characters.

The table in front of the monitor was littered with used paper cups, all with coffee dregs, and some with cigarette butts. The aluminum ashtray was filled to overflowing, but no one would get around to emptying it before the office staff showed up the next morning. There was also a pile of empty boxes from the cutlets they had delivered for dinner.

Go reached out for a pack of cigarettes, but thought better of it and put it back down. His tongue was irritated by the smoke. The editor, a man in his twenties, reached out instead and helped himself, the entire time, he, like the other two, keeping his eyes on the screen.

When Go spoke about ten minutes later, he discovered a cigarette hanging out of his mouth even though he distinctly recalled closing the pack.

"If we talk about *Ulysses*, nobody will have read it, you know. I've never read it. How about you two?"

"Not me," answered the director, a man of about forty who had been a great help to him in overseas shoots.

"But if we're doing Dublin, we'll have to have James Joyce or *Ulysses* in there somewhere."

"So let's just whisk our way through Dublin and go directly to Aran Island. We can use clips from this film and add parts of modern life, like Aran sweaters, pubs, and builders of wooden ships. Ireland has always been a European backwater, so let's focus on that aspect."

"What about the whiff of culture? All you've got on the ocean side is the smell of kelp, poverty and liquor. John Morrigan's pub, that will stand out."

"Who was that guy in *Ulysses*?"

"Bloom."

"And this was the pub that he visited? The viewers won't have any idea what it's supposed to mean. You can say this was a pub where the main character of *Ulysses* had a drink or two. Then what?"

"Don't worry about it. They wouldn't understand it even if they had read the book. The pub makes a living advertising itself as the one mentioned in *Ulysses*. That's all we have to say, it's all the visuals have to show."

"Ah, now that you mention it, I did read part of it in college. Couldn't make heads or tails out of it. It's not written so your average citizen can make sense of it."

This particular editor was a strange fellow who'd read the entire lengthy series on the legendary swordsman Musashi Miyamoto for fun in between studying for college exams, and who'd played rock music after being admitted.

"But if we mention the novel, won't we have to explain what it's about?"

"It can't be done," the editor said.

"So let's not even try. It's better to just show the place and not try to attempt something we can't follow up on."

"So we're back to the whiff of culture. P Broadcasting wants an educational program. I think we should at least mention the book."

"All right, I'll think about it during the editing process."

Go was tired, and he wanted to escape from the cigarette smoke and the sound of the air conditioner.

"The rest can wait until tomorrow." *Man of Aran* was just finishing up. A veil of fatigue had descended onto the three men, and they sluggishly stood up.

"Pay the location expenses as soon as you can, and take that bag of trash out to the corner on your way out, would you?"

After the director and editor left, Go checked his answering machine. The director of the Thursday special he was working on had left a message asking if he could have a little more leeway on the editing work he was doing in the studio Go had rented to do the job. If the offline video wasn't done on time, the video-to-video online editing would have to be delayed, and the date was already set for adding on-screen titles and doing the voiceovers. Go had already told the director that he expected the work done on time even if he had to go without sleep for three nights to do it. He paid by the day for the editing room and the performers. The show was a tour of a number of hot springs; it wasn't like the documentary on Ireland, and he couldn't afford to spend extra time on it.

In his industry Go managed two tracks, work for money and work for prestige, that he differentiated. Women, too, he distinguished, embracing some with his right arm and others with his left, as it were. Perhaps this was fine for work, but he clearly did not understand yet that this assignment of pure and impure and superior and inferior was an illusion born of simplistic thinking. Living by the idea that you need to allow the bad into yourself in order to protect the good, you frequently forget to make sure the good is still there. The truth probably is that people are driven by the pure and the impure co-existing within them chaotically, ambiguously, and indolently, but Go still believed that, when faced with an important decision in a clutch moment, he would be able without hesitation to choose the essential. If he really had to. At the crucial juncture. Beyond the wall, his true self. His brain cells still had not experienced true chaos.

There were three editing machines in one corner of Go's office; he had everything he needed here to get his work done, and the company name was displayed out front. He also rented the apartment immediately below, on the fifth floor, using it as a living room and bedroom. Up until three years before, he had only had this one apartment. He offered to rent the one below as well when he got wind of rumors that the occupant, also a production company, was headed for bankruptcy even if it discounted a bill dated six months ahead, when the program they were working on was scheduled for broadcast, and further borrowed from everyone they knew. Go had felt both a sense of superiority and compassion, but there was also the concern that this was a condominium building in Akasaka, a district where all sorts of businesses operated, and that a loud establishment could move in under his unit. There was a "love hotel" built to look like a castle in the immediate neighborhood, and he had heard that there was at least one apartment in his building used for sex work. All that felt okay at night, but whenever he hit the road outside after an all-nighter thinking about how good a sauna and a nap would feel, he realized that the unshavenness, the skin coated in the dregs of emotion and fatigue, not to mention sweat and cigarette tar, and the eating and sleeping habits completely out of sync with the rest of the civilized world, inevitably gave him the air of a rat who had just crawled out of the sewer.

He wondered if he ought to go home to Machida. He didn't do it more than once or twice a week. He always arrived late at night and slept until noon the next day. By the time he got up it was too much trouble to head back to Akasaka, so he ended up staying another night, but during his time at home he'd be faced with how smoothly his family ran without him. His wife was busy with the PTA at the schools of their children, in fifth grade and junior high, and she also served as treasurer for a Zen Buddhist organization called "Prostheses for the Children of Asia." She wasn't one to complain about not having her husband around to keep her company, and Go knew it was the result of the seeds he himself had sewn. Years ago, Go's wife had helped him edit film, and she had a good understanding of the work he did. But she looked at his business as a gamble, and he knew she was right, so they almost never talked about work at home. Compared to most men, Go was able to make do without the support of his wife. In that sense, it could be said he was independent. He didn't make waves at home; it was less trouble not to, and so, while he was never sure that his wife wanted it, he made love to her occasionally, on quiet afternoons. Besides providing for them financially, that was the one thing he did for his family.

His sons did not present their parents with any challenges. If any of them had problems, they could take care of them themselves. It was not a warm family, and this coldness kept them from deteriorating, much the way dried fish tends to last.

Go ended up back at his fifth-floor apartment, made himself a brandy and water, and drank a couple fingers before he noticed the blinking light of the answering machine on his private line.

"I'm getting used to working again. I've been able to make these changes because..."

Then the call was abruptly cut off. She must have dialed again.

"I'm sorry. Would you mind erasing that last message?"

It was after one a.m. He couldn't call Tsurugi now. She knew that this number wouldn't connect to his office, but it sounded as though she was afraid someone would overhear. *I've been able to make these changes because...* What had she planned to say next? Of what you did for me? Of the money you gave me? She might have hung up because she hadn't been able to make a decision. Had the two choices had different meanings for Chigiri? They must have, or why would she have hesitated? Or it might just have been because she heard her daughter coming downstairs.

Go Imai put down his glass and was on his way to the bathroom to take a shower when the phone rang. As soon as she had checked to make sure she had Go on the line, Chigiri spoke, in a lower voice than usual.

"I couldn't sleep, thinking about what I'd said to your answering machine. I was afraid someone might hear it; it was foolish of me."

"Huh. There was nothing recorded. Someone must have listened to it and then erased it."

"Oh no!"

"I'm kidding. Nobody heard it. If it had been something more shocking, my staff might have had a good laugh, but then they would have forgotten it. They don't care about others, and they wouldn't even remember if one day they ran into you and you reminded them of it."

"Thank goodness."

"None of them are interested in the private matters of other people."

"They're very well-mannered."

"No, just uninterested. They don't care unless it has something to do with them. It's different from the way things are in Tsurugi. Here, other men and other women can do whatever they like."

"I guess that means there's so much of that sort of thing going on, you can't keep up with each other's business. It's not even worth starting a rumor or two."

"My point is that you can leave any kind of message you like. I was glad."

"I just...just wanted to thank you again."

"For what?"

"You know, the money."

Go let out a deep sigh of disappointment, low enough that Chigiri couldn't hear. So there was no other reason why she might want to call him.

"You must have been asleep. I apologize for calling so late."

Go spoke hastily to keep her from hanging up.

"You said you'd gotten used to working. So does that mean it's not so hard for you, or does it mean you enjoy it?"

"It's not particularly fun."

"I'm having fun. I spent five hours with a film on Ireland."

"Okay, I had fun, too, listening to some of the things customers say when they're drunk."

"I wasn't really having fun. Irish people drink too much."

"I wasn't having fun either. Mayu stubbed her finger on a volleyball."

"But I'm having fun now."

"Why is that?"

"I've got someone to talk to."

"Tell me what you're looking at right now."

"What do you mean?"

"What's there in your room?"

"There's a couch. It's upholstered in brown cloth. It's got two cigarettes burns on it. There's a table with a cheap melamine finish, and I've got my feet up on it. There's a newspaper, an ashtray, a tabloid magazine, and a TV, but none of them are mine."

"Whose are they?"

"I forgot; someone left them here."

"What else is there?"

He could see his bedroom behind a glass partition. He couldn't decide whether to mention it.

"There's a glass partition, with a...picture hung on it."

"What's the picture of?"

"Scenery."

Now that was a lie. It was a poster of two girls in bikinis waving a checkered flag at a car, but Go had no recollection of taping it up there. It must have been a client.

"I don't believe you about the scenery."

"Okay, it's a poster of a car."

"Now that's a lie, too. If it were a car, you would have said so right away. It's got to be something embarrassing."

"There are two girls in swimsuits next to the car."

"Come on…"

"I swear, that's the truth."

The harder Go tried to convince her, the more she laughed at him. He realized what she must have in mind, and he finally gave up trying. A cool breeze came in through the window and he felt himself calming down.

"Does this happen to you often?"

"What do you mean?" she asked.

"Things that aren't there are somewhere inside of you; and the opposite too."

"I don't know what you mean. You must be drinking."

"As soon as I'm done with this job, I'm going back to see you." There, he said it.

"I see." Chigiri's voice suddenly went demure. Go could see the serious look in her eyes as she got ready to do her duty, and he panicked.

"This time I want you to stay with me until night." He refused to give up.

"I understand."

"No you don't."

Now he was angry.

But the truth was that he didn't understand, either.

Chigiri was sure Go was saying he wanted to see her because that picture on the wall had put the idea into his head. She wasn't sure whether his forceful attitude bothered or excited her, but she decided she shouldn't react to them, and chose her words carefully.

"I do understand. And I'll be waiting for you, so let me know when you've set a date."

Her voice was as polite and devoid of emotion as a woman taking reservations at a hotel desk. She wanted to add that he should ask much more of her this time—it was his right to do so. But to her credit, she didn't.

7

IT WAS MID-JULY, a few days before the date Go Imai had set to see Chigiri again. She was working at Manraku, a sushi shop, and overheard the owner chatting with a customer with whom he had plans to go mountain-stream fishing the next day. Chigiri finally had to butt in and ask what the "fly" in "fly fishing" meant. They explained that it referred to the lures they used that looked like real bait: the ant-lion, water moth, and water fly were all insects that hatched in the water, and then got their wings on the water surface. Nishimura, the customer, explained that they were the main food for the freshwater salmon and char. Her boss Tokiyama, wrapping up his knives for the night, went on to tell her that they would choose lures that looked like insects that developed about this time of year. The water moth bred all year round, did she know that? Chigiri was pretty sure she must have seen one, but she certainly didn't remember it.

Amused at her interest, Nishimura invited her to come along with them the next day. They were going to a place called Akadan.

"It's easier to understand if you can get a look—if you don't mind wading up the river, that is." Tokiyama added that he had a spare pair of waders, and smilingly encouraged her to join their party.

Deep inside the mountains, Akadan or Red Valley was accessed from the hamlet of Motokuwashima, an hour's drive upstream along the Tedorigawa. What was more mountain stream than river at that point

97

flowed from deep inside the valley. The gravel road that ran upstream along the flow from Motokuwashima accommodated no more than a single car; beyond where the road ended was a brook occluded in a dark forest of trees, where there was no space even to fling out a fishing rod.

Naturally, though Chigiri had grown up in Tsurugi, she'd never ventured so far into the mountains, and fishermen and bear hunters did not foray so deep, either, unless something other than catch, some mystical passion, lured them.

The men had casually invited her, and she had just as casually accepted. She had been drawn by the discussion of the water insects, which they had described as living treasures, so tiny and difficult to handle, easily blown away by the slightest puff of breath. To Chigiri their enthusiasm was as appealing as that of two small boys, but the other reason she accepted was that she was in a state of high anticipation to see Go again. And she had promised to stay with him until night. What else could make a fly-fishing expedition sound like so much fun?

Neither Nishimura nor Tokiyama were in the habit of taking women along on their trips. They had both publicly declared that females could never appreciate the joys of their favorite hobby. They had obviously asked Chigiri along because they liked her—they wouldn't have described it as a physical attraction, but they couldn't necessarily swear that that wasn't it either. It was a vague sort of situation, but it involved little danger. As for Chigiri, she had never associated with men before in a manner that could be described as platonic, and she was starving for it. Both Nishimura and Tokiyama knew about her divorce and her invalid father, but they didn't pry into her personal life. Tokiyama, the owner of Manraku, was almost sixty, while Nishimura, more than a dozen years younger, was an osteopath in his mid-forties.

The next morning at five, Nishimura picked up Chigiri and Tokiyama in his SUV from in front of the sushi shop. As instructed, Chigiri was dressed in jeans and a long-sleeved shirt. She wore jeans she had borrowed from Mayu, complete with a hole in the knee. She had made rice balls for the group for lunch, filling them with salty pickled plums and wasabi leaves, because the men said it was the easiest thing to eat while fishing.

They drove as high as Shiramine-honson along Tedorigawa, so that much was familiar to Chigiri, but when they reached Akadan, the road all but disappeared, and the skeleton mascot Nishimura had dangling from his rearview mirror danced and clattered as they drove over the uneven surface. The party was in danger of hitting their heads on the ceiling of the car every time it hit a hole.

After about half an hour of this, just as Chigiri's buttocks were beginning to hurt, the car came to a stop in a clearing and Tokiyama declared "let's start here" in high spirits, handing Chigiri a pair of waders. She put them on, and they came up to her chest. By the time she was ready, Tokiyama and Nishimura were also covered in black rubber that squished and squeaked as they walked around the car, getting their poles and bait ready.

They walked down to the stream from the car, picking their way carefully over rocks from which kudzu vines had crept and spread out. It was slowgoing as they put forward one rubber-shod sole after another. Nishimura and Tokiyama got down first, and were already in the water by the time Chigiri arrived.

Nishimura stood in front with his line bent like a whip. The line was a thick fishing line coated with plastic, two or three millimeters in diameter. Attached to that was the leader, a thinner line. Before Chigiri had a chance to see the lures and guess which insects they represented, the two men were deep into the stream. Chigiri, eager to keep up, waded as quickly as she could over the rocks in the streambed, but was careful not to make too much noise. The two men worked in sync, first one then the other stepping forward to fling his line upstream.

The lure was evidently landing where it was intended, and then pulled up after it had floated several feet downstream. The line made a large half circle over the surface of the river and parallel to it, and the tip landed on a single spot. During the instant that the breeze kept the long line off the water surface, it was dyed a golden color, catching the diffused reflection of the sun, still just over the horizon and poking its way through the trees and onto the water.

To Chigiri, the sparkling line and the even-thinner leader looked like the soft strands of a spider's web floating in the air. The river, she felt, was a living, flowing being caressed by the delicate, silk-like thread. Just at that instant, something lifted up out of the shadow of the riverbed, then leaped off of the river surface, flipping backwards and shining white. It slid over the surface of the water and into the waiting hands of Nishimura. By the time Chigiri had moved closer to see it, the first catch of the day had already been delivered back to the river, a black shadow quickly gone. Nishimura explained that they always let the first fish go.

For the next hour or so, Chigiri followed the two up the river. They took a break at the first bridge they came to, and she got her first good look at the bait. Tokiyama's lure was a water moth made of the hair of a deer. Nishimura's was the same, but slightly smaller. After a smoke, Tokiyama took his fly box out of his fishing vest, and pulled out an even smaller water moth. Chigiri peeked over at the box to see a large number of lures, all neatly arranged.

Nishimura asked Chigiri if her feet weren't cold. Still enthralled by the experience, she responded that she hadn't given her feet a second thought. She didn't feel cold so much as lost.

When she told Go about the trip, he was brought up short by the word "lost." This prevented Chigiri from going any further with her story.

"I don't understand what you mean by 'lost.'" From the ninth floor of the hotel he could look out at the faded violet of the western sky. The violet was quickly going gray, and then mulberry-colored.

"We just kept going, further and further into a place I didn't know."

"If you were going upstream, it meant you were heading into the mountains, right?"

"It was like a hunt. Men, hunting."

Still facing the window, Go turned his head. Chigiri was sitting on the side of the bed, leaning back on her arms. Her knees were slightly open, and the leg below her knees went straight down to the floor, with her ankles open just a little wider than her knees. The green flared skirt barely covering her knees flowed out to the right and left. From where Go stood, the place beyond those knees was deep and dark. He tried not to stare at those depths, brushing past them to look into Chigiri's eyes.

"Of course it's not a hunt."

"It looked like one to me. Imagine being hooked like that. There would be no escape."

"Sounds desperate."

"It was. It was a hunt to the death."

"I wish you could see your eyes. You look like a fish trying to escape. But lots of them *do* escape, don't they?"

"The lure comes floating down, aimed at a spot where there are likely to be fish. I couldn't bear it. It wasn't like a harpoon or spear. Fish would be able to avoid that. They go after them by landing ever so softly on the water. If there happens to be a fish right there, it doesn't have a chance."

Chigiri's face glowed. She had a fever in her eyes and perspiration around her nose. Go could feel the fever, but the heat he felt was jealousy, although he wasn't yet aware of it yet. What he did notice was her knees inching apart.

"I tell you, they were hunting. They headed up the river; said they were thrilled wondering what might be ahead or around a bend. They couldn't help themselves from going in deeper and deeper."

"And you felt lost?"

"That's right. You can't keep water from flowing from its source. Do you understand what I'm saying, Go? The need to keep going in deeper and further in? They said any man would understand."

"How old is this Nishimura?"

"Maybe forty-five or six. He's an osteopath. He said when he looks at people, he doesn't see their skin; he sees straight through to their bones. He said it wasn't like that when he was young, but now when he sees a naked woman, all he can see is her skeleton."

"Now that's a lie. But I do understand the need to keep going in. I don't know about fly fishing, but I get the gist."

"Because you're a man?"

As she asked this, she moved her knees unconsciously. She looked down at her feet, and noticed that a deep hollow like that red valley had crawled in under her skirt. She put pressure on both her knees, this time consciously. Akadan grew sharply deeper. She felt as if the sake she'd had at dinner was passing through her stomach and seeping out from the deepest recesses of Akadan. Chigiri was aware of her arousal, yet desired at the same time to make Go just stand by that window.

Go didn't answer Chigiri's question, he just stared at her. His attitude made her feel deliciously uneasy, while her restlessness had him in impatient agony, resulting in a brief, or was it a long, period of silence.

They were both thinking about the same thing, but from different positions. Chigiri was at the top of the mountain peering down at the deep valley between her legs and, beyond that, at her slippered feet, which felt oddly detached from the rest of her body. Go was standing at the foot of the mountain gazing up deep inside the valley, waiting for the right moment to start the trek in.

He was beginning to understand what she meant by feeling lost. Even the part about the hunt was making sense. Add to that her feeling of being lost while in the company of two men—now he had to admit he was jealous. He wanted to say he'd like to visit this sushi shop, this Manraku, but he couldn't. He was so confused about how he felt that he ended up saying something generous.

"Well, I'm glad to hear you've met some nice people at that sushi shop."

"Yes, indeed." Chigiri slowly crossed her legs. Now she felt as if Go had abandoned her.

"Didn't you say the owner was a friend of Matsuko's?"

"That's right. A handsome man with one of those close, square haircuts. When he holds the trout he's caught in his hand, they stop flopping around. He's very kind; I was lucky to get a job with him." Chigiri wasn't lying, but she hadn't mentioned his age or that the masculine hairstyle was completely gray.

Women are skilled at picking and choosing from the information they have on hand, divulging only the parts that are to their own advantage. Men create illusions out of the information they receive, and steel themselves against them. This was what was happening to Chigiri and Go at this moment, and it was similar to the long-distance phone call when the discussion turned to the poster on the glass partition in Go's apartment. Their positions were now just the opposite, but Go was unable to remember that night. Just as Chigiri had evoked images of something overtly sexual on the wall of his apartment, Go had painted a picture of a man a few years younger than himself, one with healthy skin and a gentle, wholesome demeanor, standing behind the pristine white counter of a sushi bar. He was glad she was working for a good man, and he meant what he said.

Even when adult men and women are unable to say what is really in their hearts, they are able to perform as if they are doing so. The real pros are able to tell the difference, accepting or rejecting what they hear without letting on that they know, but they can only do it if they are not deeply in love with or even strongly attracted to the other party. The trick is to view the situation with a cool, detached eye.

On this particular evening, Chigiri was neither calm nor detached, and she was unable to read beyond the words Go spoke. All she could think about was how his favoring her was part and parcel of the money he had given her. She was determined not to lose sight of this fact or reveal any uneasiness. She looked down and muttered that it was all thanks to him that things were working out for her, and indicated that they might as well get moving with their plans for the evening.

"I can't just sit here; I've got to take a shower first."

"You don't have to yet—well, do whatever you like."

Go watched Chigiri disappear into the bathroom and heard the sound of the shower. He was glad that the money had been useful to her, but it had created an obstacle in their relationship. At the same time, he almost wished he had given her twice as much so she wouldn't have had to take the job at the sushi shop. But then he remembered that she had wanted to leave the house and get a job—it was the life she had wanted for herself. What was it that *he* wanted from her?

You could say that he struggled, the sound of the shower pounding him. As for Chigiri, standing in the bathtub with the water flowing over her shoulders, the only thing she could think of was that she wanted to feel her skin against Go's. She wanted him to feel pleasure, and she wanted to feel half the pleasure that she would give him. Half the pleasure Go would feel would be enough to shatter her world. But even if she felt the ground crumbling from underneath her, she would be careful not to cry out too loudly. She ground her teeth together just thinking about it.

The shower made her nipples rigid and she used the water to clean out the sticky liquid flowing from deep inside her, but its force merely stimulated a new flow. Chigiri was afraid that this would repulse Go, so she thrust her fingers inside to try to clean it all out only to find herself in the dark depths of Akadan where something frightening lived, and she quickly pulled them out again.

Sexual love was sexual love; that was all it was. It took up no more than a few moments of a human life. In ancient times, it had to be done while beating drums to keep wild beasts at bay; now, in a civilized world, more time could be spent enjoying it. But then again, when you compared it to the amount of time spent eating, sleeping and moving, humans only spent the briefest amount of time enjoying this natural instinct. Although, when you get down to it, humans don't have truly functional instincts. It might be better to say "in disobedience of natural instinct," seeing as they pursue sexual love in all seasons and well past the age of procreation.

The degree of ecstasy resulting from acts of passion that fly in the face of instinct is not something that can be shared with another person. Nor can you save it up and store it for later, the way you might make and bottle jam from an overabundance of apples.

People can be controlled by the pleasure that comes and goes during the act itself because sexual pleasure spreads from the genitals throughout the psyche, and humans are capable of recalling memories of it. This too is a result of malfunctioning instincts.

The sensations Go and Chigiri shared in bed that night could not be described as an explosion, a flood or a collapse. There was suppression which their memories doubled, and internal pressure that increased the swells. The suppression caused sorrow and greatly influenced their lives later on because both of them left unsaid the things they most wanted to say to each other.

Rather than facing Go with the questions she had for him, Chigiri put on a cheery face and returned to bed. Her eyes were as bright and moist as those of a child overexcited and broken out in a fever. Go, in turn, felt forced to mischievously express his own joy as he spoke to Chigiri wrapped in a bath towel and sitting in a formal position on the bed.

"That's a bad habit you've got of sitting like that. I think I'll have a shower before my feast, too."

By the time he returned, neither of them was smiling. *Forget the money,* he wanted to beg, but he knew it would have the opposite effect of what he wanted. Chigiri had her own voice running amok. *Don't hold back on me, don't look at me like you owe me.*

Why did it have to be like this, Go wondered. He had been looking forward to this moment. Why did it have to be so ceremonial? Here they were again, right on time and correctly in place, he thought as he slowly pushed her down.

Chigiri regretted using the word "prostitute" the last time they were together, but right now her body was so sensitive and her senses so full that she had no alternative but to follow Go's lead, and obediently fell back.

Their lips joined, their tongues entangled, and to the degree that this simple repetitive action made it impossible to see each other's faces, their ulterior motives and consciousness receded, replaced by barefaced desire. They forgot to brood over what the other might be thinking, satisfied at proof that the other's desire matched their own. This was the stage of sexual love. All it took was the contact of lips and tongues to get them that far.

As soon as Chigiri was satisfied of Go's desire for her, and Go understood Chigiri's intentions, they both got bolder. Go's fingers ventured down low, and Chigiri opened her legs a few inches to allow him entrance to go as deeply as he liked. Go's fingers were sucked in by the folds, a graceful intruder, rubbing and exerting a little pressure here and then there, experimenting to see how Chigiri's body would react. Go's fingers were audacious, but his expression was that of a philosopher or martyr, with a touch of agony. He searched Chigiri's countenance, looking for something more than sexual desire for him, although the search was difficult to conduct objectively as his own temperature rose and clouded his brain. But when his fingers got a reaction, he closed his eyes to slits; his only view a hazy shot of Chigiri's nose and lips. Her nostrils twitched, and her lips began to dry from the force of air gasping in and out. When he heard from deep inside her throat her pathetic attempt to control her breath, he employed a second finger in order to hold the soft bulge inside the folds and manipulate it. Chigiri's breath burst out in a single blast along with a sharp cry that hit Go in the face.

Go knew from experience that Chigiri had been trying to control her reaction. But it was only possible with her voice and upper body. His fingers told him that if she tried to control her lower body, it would eventually melt from the heat, something that was exactly the opposite of her intentions.

Go whispered in her ear.

"You don't have to pretend you don't feel it."

Her eyes opened a crack and her voice came out from her quickly drying lips.

"I made up my mind—I'll be satisfied with half the pleasure I give you."

"Forget the half bit. Instead let's say I'll feel it twice as strongly as you."

They smiled at each other as best they could in that position.

"Nobody's ever done this to me before."

"You mean with the fingers?"

"I've got to remember it. I want to remember everything, so give me more."

"You mean like this?"

"Now I know."

"What do you know?"

"How many, many women, you, Go, how many. . .you've done this with."

Her voice was no more than a succession of sighs, wind that was trapped between each word. Her lower body was releasing an excess of electricity that came up through her throat. Their attempt at conversation took up all their excess air, and there was less and less of it as the conversation continued while their actions picked up speed, until they could manage no more than a jumble of word endings. Go finally put his mouth over Chigiri's, a sign that she needn't talk anymore. He was a despotic and self-sacrificing pillager. He was also an explorer going further into the mountain, upstream along the Akadan river.

Go was using both hands to open up the valley two other men had taken her to. Chigiri waited breathlessly for the man now about to enter her. She felt like an enormous mountain. Each felt as though their own body as well as that of the other was a vast unmoving thing. Just as Go prepared to penetrate the valley, just as he slowly began his invasion, they both felt something tight and sharp, and cried out in what was almost pain.

The ancient exercise, the orgasm for which, at that point, anything was to be sacrificed. Starting out as creatures with misguided instincts, yet they had no choice but to fall into that involuntary muscle spasm that all other creatures have known. It wasn't in perfect coordination; Chigiri came a few seconds ahead, but was still falling to earth after Go had landed. Go was the one who understood this, not Chigiri.

Chigiri remembered Go's promise to her.

"So did you feel twice as good as I did?"

"Yeah."

"Really?"

Chigiri's forehead was covered in sweat, and there were lines between her eyebrows, making her look even more childish than usual. Go nodded with conviction in his eyes. If it had been true, if she had only had half his pleasure, he would have been unable to forgive himself. On the other hand, imagining she had felt twice or three times as good didn't make sense either.

They lay on their backs staring up at the ceiling. A smoke sensor stuck out of the bright gray-green expanse like a belly button. Looking straight across toward the door, the square mouth of the air conditioner was wide open, cold air coming out of it. All of a sudden, Chigiri was convinced that the square mouth and the bulging sensor in the ceiling were a camera and microphone positioned to spy on their naked bodies. Go looked at them, too, but only to note that they were old-fashioned devices, completely different from the newer models in any hotel in Akasaka or Roppongi. He also thought, in his post-ejaculatory languor, that his relationship with Chigiri was old-fashioned—the manuals he'd followed for other interpersonal relationships should work, he did need to do something. Since their second act had left both of them satisfied, Go's thoughts were growing lazy. *When you made love to women, they would be like this or like that.* It wasn't clear in his mind exactly what he meant, but Chigiri had not proved to be an exception to his personal experience, he thought as he began to doze off.

He was still blissfully relaxed, when Chigiri, also in a half-conscious state, spoke in the delighted tone of voice a child might use when chasing after a puppy.

"When I remember that night at Heisenji, I always try to get that feeling again. But I never can because I keep seeing your face. It kills the mood. You've put some kind of a curse on me."

"A curse?"

"Like you're refusing to let me feel the pleasure unless you're there with me."

Go was at a loss. No woman had ever talked to him about such an intimate act before, and needless to say, none had mentioned that they saw his face while they were doing it, or that visions of his face had subdued their excitement. He felt simultaneously provoked and rejected, and couldn't come up with a reply.

"So I kill the mood?"

"Yes. I wonder why?"

"It's not a curse. You're... you're..."

"I know, I know. I'm thinking about you too much."

Things were not getting any clearer to Go.

"So whose face would keep you excited? Those two guys?"

"What guys?"

"The ones who took you to Akadan."

Chigiri giggled, still feeling deliciously drowsy, while Go was now wide awake.

"You've got it wrong," she mumbled.

"So what *do* you mean? I don't turn you off completely, I know that. Just now, and that night at the Kimura place, you came with no problem."

"That's right, but it's an embarrassing topic, so let's drop it."

Go was not prepared to drop the conversation. He sat up and lit a cigarette. Chigiri had only been honest with him; how could she know the state of confusion she had set him up for? She didn't realize that she had destroyed his few moments of post-coital peace. She had wanted to tell him that late at night, when she was alone and needed to feel that pleasure again, she couldn't complete the act without his skin on hers. She hadn't considered her words; she was relaxed and satisfied and had left them to take care of themselves.

Go rubbed Chigiri's eyelids and forehead, still covered in sweat. He couldn't resort to his usual way of dealing with people after all; she no longer fit into his formula of women after he had made love to them.

He had seen himself as climbing up the river into Akadan. He was the invader. How could he have foreseen that the mountain itself would draw him in and drink him up? He had set on his journey beginning with sex, only to find himself at the peak of both a psychological and spiritual mountain.

"I feel like water is flowing under the bed," Chigiri said. Go couldn't tell by looking at her, as she muttered and shook her head, if the evening's passion had changed her or not, but he, too, could hear the sound of water. It ran from his foot to his head, creating little bumps and ripples along the path.

At eleven on the dot, Chigiri left for home, just as she had announced when they met at dinner. She refused to let him see her off, but accepted the taxi fare he had put in an envelope for her, said good night, and left with a polite nod of her head.

Left alone, Go was still wide awake. He took a bottle of whiskey from the minibar and began to sip it. Chigiri hopped in the taxi without a second thought, leaving all her thoughts to the summer night. About the time the taxi passed by the Rokuro Cedar, she suddenly came back to her senses. Had Mayu eaten dinner? Would she believe her story about meeting some old friends at Korinbo? She looked out around her, and in turning her head discovered the remains of the warmth of Go's arm around her, supporting her head.

8

GO IMAI VISITED CHIGIRI three more times that summer and fall. Work usually prevented him from leaving Tokyo during September and early October, so he went at the end of o-bon during the hottest part of August, once in October, and once in mid-November, when the oak and plane trees turned red and yellow, creating colors so brilliant that they seemed to be in fierce competition with the deep blue sky. Three times he made the long trip from Tokyo, and met her in Kanazawa or Tsurugi, and they made love. In November, he went to the hospital to see Kaho. Afterwards they went to her home in Chimori. Mayu was on an overnight school trip and it was still early, so they stayed there and made love in her room on her bed. Then they drove to Kanazawa for dinner, and ended up once again in Go's hotel room for another few hours of carnal pleasure.

Back in Tokyo, Go couldn't get the impression of Chigiri's room out of his head. Nor the specter of Kaho who could not remember Go's visit nine months before. He was convinced Go was the spirit of a thief from hundreds of years ago. For his part, Go was startled to see how Kaho's dementia had worsened and how he had shrunken physically.

"Even thieves have a line they won't cross," Kaho began to pontificate. "I stole Tedorigawa water from Iguchi, and I posted my brothers in Okuwa, Tosaka, and Matsuto, and their sons in Yasuda, Yamagami, and Yokoe, but I refused to steal the holy water from Hakusan. That holy water was a treasure and had the power to send off the Heike reinforcements troops of Yoshinaka.

"And where do you draw your line? If you insist on taking my daughter with you to thieve, then take these two swords and five daggers with you. If you have no principles, they won't do you much good, but they are much too heavy for an old man like me..."

Chigiri, standing at the head of his bed, did her best to keep from laughing. Every time Go tried to get a word in, she put a finger to her lips begging him with her eyes to let her father say whatever he liked.

Go found it difficult to feel as playful about the accusations as Chigiri, and he listened to them earnestly. He began to feel as though he were a thief, and wondered what about his nature had made him that way.

He went on, somewhat superfluously, to wonder whether Kaho was pretending to have lost his mind and actually meant what he said. He knew that dementia could come and go, and if the old man had any notion that his hospital room was being paid for by the man standing before him, a man who was sleeping with his daughter, he might not be able to speak his mind without hiding behind the veil of insanity.

As for the house in Chimori, Kaho's bedding had been replaced in the living room with a *kotatsu*, an old-fashioned foot heater. The scene stuck in Go's mind vividly, and even after he was back in Tokyo working, he occasionally took himself back there. In his mind he was standing in that room again. The heater had been covered with a generic, red plastic table, and the calligraphy for "cloud" was still over the Shinto shrine.

He had opened the door to her room, and as soon as he saw her sofa bed spread out in it, he'd impulsively grabbed her and lay her down on it to kiss her. She'd asked him to wait a moment, jumped up, hurried to the front door and locked it. This was one of the parts he remembered and replayed endlessly, but what remained glued most firmly in his memory was the character for "cloud," and the make-believe that there were nothing but clouds above it.

Now we can walk over that area as much as we like.

She had explained on his prior visit the resourcefulness with which her family had build the two-story house. She hadn't explained it again, but he could hear her voice repeating the explanation. It was as if those words described the difficult part of their relationship, and with every recollection he felt a wish to dispel the word "cloud" from his memory.

In the end he wondered why he was having melancholy thoughts and why, despite them, his blood was coursing wildly through his veins. Confusion? Bitter regret? And what was it that he regretted? He could hunt down the answer to that question, but that would only exacerbate the bitterness.

Why had he given Chigiri that money so casually? One wrong step at the watershed sent you tumbling down the wrong slope, away from the sea you were heading for.

Getting off the elevator, in the Akasaka building, and stepping out onto the solid concrete, he saw a few flyers on the floor. Someone must have taken them out of a mailbox on the first floor. On one of them was a photo of ten nude women all lined up. Each of them had a name and a telephone number written prominently beneath. There it was, sex available for anyone who could pay for it. It made Go feel even more depressed, but oddly stimulated, too. He felt masochistic—why not scoop up all the flyers and buy himself a woman? But instead he merely walked over the flyers, pulling his office key out of his pocket.

If he had demonstrated his feelings for Chigiri through his attitudes and words, or with a gaze, or his entire body—if he had stated his emotions for her and then been rejected and still gone on to take the time and effort... If he had been humiliated, gotten angry and then consoled himself, and had finally had a physical relationship with her... If, after all that, they had been able to relate to each other as individuals equally attracted to each other, *that* would have been the moment when he could have given her the money. If he had done it all in the correct order he wouldn't be regretting anything now.

It hadn't been merely a financial transaction, but he had done it as casually as he had trod on the flyers of the women scattered on the concrete. He was getting his just deserts for all of the women he had been with in the past. Forty-seven years of life had resulted in a fatal mistake of order.

He clearly remembered offering Chigiri the money. They had been talking on the phone, not looking into each other's faces, and it had slipped out. He would have been too embarrassed to do it any other way. While it hadn't been a completely false front, he never would have been able to say anything like that face-to-face. And he'd had a drink. He never suspected she would answer as she did. And now all of this regret had followed.

Three of his editors were in the office when he arrived. They had finished the sound on a video and had just returned from the editing studio and were eating a lunch they'd had delivered. An hour later, Go took them all to a bar in Akasaka-mitsuke that featured Caucasian hostesses. The two who came to their table could only speak a little Japanese. The innocuous arena of fun that came into being precisely because it precluded communication was filled with jokes in stilted English, the sparkling pale skin of their companions, and "Because" by the Dave Clark Five.

Because, because, I love you.

Go went to the restroom, urinated, and washed his hands. There were small artificial flowers wrapped around the faucet over the urinal, and water flowed from it. He had to admit that he was in love with Chigiri. He stood there in unsteady, drunken thought trying to figure out a way to start their relationship over. Eventually the door opened behind him; one of his staff was checking to make sure he was all right. "Because" came flying in and landed on his head. Go fell on his ass. He wasn't that drunk; it was as though the post inside him holding him up had broken in two. His companion hoisted him up, commenting that he hadn't looked well lately, and should really see a doctor.

At the same time, Chigiri Yamazaki was sitting at the counter of Manraku eating *chirashi-zushi* prepared by the owner, Tokiyama. The last customer had left, and Chigiri had cleaned up the upstairs room and was taking off her apron when Tokiyama offered to make her the dish of sushi rice covered with ingredients leftover from the evening. Chigiri was in the habit of eating dinner at home before stopping in at the hospital and heading to work. She wasn't particularly hungry but thought she'd enjoy a little conversation with Tokiyama, so she gratefully accepted.

Tokiyama put a layer of *kanpyo*, shiitake, and sweet omelet strips over the rice, and quickly covered it with leftover bits of octopus, squid, and shrimp, and put it out on the counter for her. Chigiri made herself some tea, took her chopsticks and dug in. Tokiyama sipped some heated sake as he lit a cigarette. Still dressed in his white, starched shirt and apron, and with his thin, sharp-boned face and short and silver haircut, he looked wiry and masculine. Chigiri liked Tokiyama's disheveled smile, with its hint of age and fatigue.

"Mr. Tokiyama, you have completely different expressions on your face when you're holding a carving knife, a fishing pole, and a cigarette," said Chigiri as she gathered a few shreds of omelet together with her chopsticks. At relaxed times like these, Tokiyama always gave her the feeling she could talk about just about anything.

"How about a drink?" was his response.

"Don't mind if I do."

Chigiri went for a sake cup and held it out for him to fill.

"How's your father?"

"Pretty funny. He's still making me laugh."

Tokiyama smiled in return.

"The other day he thought he was Hayashi Rokuro-Mitsuaki. You know the Rokuro Cedar from the Genji-Heike..."

"Yup, I remember."

"He made secret negotiations with a Heike faction, and dashed on horseback to the camp of Kiso Yoshinaka."

"Rokuro-Mitsuaki died in a battle won using the 'burning cow' strategy, didn't he?"

"Is that right? My father's one-man performances haven't got that far yet."

"They wrapped the horns and tails of hundreds of cows in oiled paper, set them on fire and let the animals loose. The cows, in their pain and terror, thundered toward the walls of the castle."

"I'll have to watch out for that one. The man sharing my father's room has a bad heart, I'm not sure he could survive cows on fire. My father's stories are too realistic for comfort sometimes."

"I'd like to hear them."

"Dementia means setting your heart free from reality. At least he's enjoying the life of a hero—for now. I'm younger than my father, but I've been having some problems keeping my feet on the ground lately. It might be early-onset dementia."

As she spoke, Chigiri gave no hint of unease. Indeed, she seemed to yearn for a world where she could live out her dreams. Her wistful premonition would eventually come true, but that time was still a long way off. For now, it was no more than a tiny seed deep inside the creases of her childlike smile.

"Mr. Tokiyama, can you tell me the difference between love and the desire of a man to have sex with a woman?"

Tokiyama, cigarette between his lips, narrowed his eyes at the question. To Chigiri it made him look more like a boy than a man approaching sixty. Tokiyama had been so astonished by the word "sex" that he had not heard the rest of the question.

Chigiri knew it was not a question appropriate to the occasion, but she had been asking it of herself over and over and could not come up with an answer. Unable to decide whether she should just drop it, she leaned over and asked him again, this time in a lower voice.

"That's a tough one," Tokiyama managed to sputter out without looking too embarrassed. He was puzzled by her words, but also oddly, and somewhat discomfitedly, aroused by them. "Have you been having some problems?"

"Yes. I mean, no."

"If you use the word 'sex' in front of a man, you're going to provoke him, you know."

"Really?"

"Of course, I'm too old for that."

In the end, Chigiri's question went unanswered, but nor did Tokiyama make her feel like a fool for asking. Chigiri considered Tokiyama a good man, but not someone she would rely on in an emergency. Tokiyama felt that Chigiri was a little "different," but noticed that her eccentricity kept her from drawing the attention of undesirable men.

She put on her coat and went outside. The half moon was shining brightly in the night sky. She walked in the opposite direction of her home in Chimori, stopping outside the hospital. She counted the windows on the third floor, locating her father's room. She assured herself that the lights were out and he was asleep. Then she backtracked towards home.

Listening to the sound of water running through the irrigation ditch on the eastern side of the hospital she could tell the snow season was close at hand. She headed towards Togashi Bridge on the path along the ditch. The white light of the moon wended its way up the surface of the water. At some points the light shattered like shards of ice. Following the road to the right from Togashi Bridge, she looked up at the moon again. This was what she always did, and she always thought of Go.

This evening, however, was different. She remembered the conversation of two workers from the local ironworks who came in still in their uniforms. They looked to be in their mid-thirties, and gave her a diligent, upright impression. She unwittingly listened in on their conversation as she cleaned up some other tables.

You say I'm just messing around? Can you really claim it's not romance if you pay for it? I'm just buying myself a little love. Love and crime aren't just separated by a thin line, they overlap. I don't want a woman, I just want one night of romance.

The other man laughed, and told him he was fooling himself.

It was the first time it had occurred to Chigiri that what she had might not be called love or romance. She naturally didn't agree with the first man, but she was brought up short by the other who laughed at him. She felt as if she'd happened onto some kind of truth, and that was why she had asked Tokiyama the question about sex.

As she walked accompanied by the moon, she thought about how nice it would be if she could be as honest as the man who had been chided by his friend.

She had received the money from Go, and then he had made love to her. She had tried to tell herself it was duty, nothing more than a job, but the truth was that she wanted him to hold her in his arms, and it had nothing to do with the money. She was in love with him and was using the money to hide behind, to protect herself from getting hurt.

Maybe a little explanation can shed light on how Chigiri felt and whether money can be used to avoid pain. It goes without saying that women the world over continue to be hurt by the money they accept for the use of their bodies. Self-respect and ego are wounded long before there is any physical injury. Money is paid as compensation for all of this.

But Chigiri was different. She could foresee the pain of losing the joy of being loved and desired wholeheartedly. Understanding someone's enormous presence incites the fear of losing the same. Thus, Chigiri had built a dike of money to protect herself. If she lost Go, she would feel less pain if she could convince herself that it had been no more than a monetary transaction between man and woman.

She realized, as she walked under the moon that night, how petty she had been. There was another, physical element of the case that bears mention. Not only had Chigiri failed to be a "prostitute" during their first encounter, but any free moment found her recalling Go's lips, the sensation of his lips on her nipples, the warmth of the blood circulating in his erection when he was inside of her.

If that was all, she might not disqualify, but she was also constantly yearning to put her face in the hollow of his neck and shoulder so she could feel his heat and drink in his smell. She'd remember her nose and mouth buried in him and how she tried to twist in further. She'd remember it and imagine doing it again, and want to burst out in tears. *That* was when she lost her license as a prostitute.

That night, much later, Chigiri got a call from Go. She picked up the receiver, and as soon as she heard his voice, turned on the kerosene stove. She knew that huddling with the phone in the kitchen would have her chilled to the bone in no time, and she counted on his calls lasting at least half an hour. Go was drunk. His drunken voice came through as clearly as the droplets of water dripping out of the kitchen faucet they had to leave on all night to keep the pipes from freezing solid. An aluminum pan had been placed under the faucet to keep the sound of the water quiet. When it was full, the water skirted by the cup and spoon coated with the residue of instant coffee before traveling down the drain.

The night visitors in this home were Go and the constantly dripping faucet.

"I just got home. It's cold. It must be cold in Tsurugi."

"I just turned on the heater."

"Tonight, I went to a bar with foreign hostesses and fell on my ass in the men's room."

"Is something wrong?"

"Something, all over. There's something wrong."

"...There's a half moon tonight. It looks good enough to eat."

"What?"

"Never mind."

"Is it waxing or waning?"

"What?"

"The moon. You were talking about the moon, weren't you?"

"The moon? I'm not sure. I think it's waxing."

"I hope so. That'll make you happy for a while."

"...A while?"

"After the full moon, it gets smaller."

"Now you're making me sad."

"I suppose I can see the moon here, too. The Akasaka moon is probably red."

"If you say so."

"I'm drunk."

Neither of them laughed. They were getting soaked in a damp fog of sorrow. And at the very depths of both of their sorrow was something akin to fear, lying quietly on its side. For a few moments they pulled each other into an unknown territory in their mutual silence.

Go spoke first. "There's something important I need to say, but I don't have the right words. I don't want to say anything that other people have said. But I can't figure out how to do it."

"It's all right."

"I'll do something about us."

"...Today one of the customers said something interesting. He said he paid women for sex, but during the time they were doing it, it was love. The guy he was with said there was no romance involved when you paid for it. So which do you think it is? Is it love?"

"Probably..."

"Probably what?"

"Probably it's an excuse either way."

"Either way?"

"It's either a hypocritical excuse to believe that it's not prostitution and that somehow their hearts have been linked. Either that, or he's embarrassed that he really did like the girl. The first type is the most common, I guess, but it's scary. It makes you wonder what sort of animals we humans are."

"Can you call it love if you buy a woman and are with her only once?"

"There are men and women who are together for twenty years and never have love or romance. If that guy thought it was romance, then it was. It was his love affair."

Go, what about us? Chigiri almost said it, but couldn't.

Go understood that she had nearly stepped into that place that scared her so. He responded with something more daring and direct.

"I want you. I want you right now."

Chigiri toppled from the cliff she was so precariously balanced on.

"Do you think we can see each other before New Year's?"

Electric Christmas decorations made a whirlpool of light on the walls of buildings and at the entrances to hotels. The first snow of the year had melted, and it was proving to be a warm December for Kanazawa. Go and Chigiri walked among the night lights from Katamachi to the old samurai homes in Nagamachi and back again. They had been wondering around for about thirty minutes. They ended up down the road at Omicho Market and looked at the Echizen crabs, yellowtail, and salmon roe all shining beautifully under the bright lights, and they were both ready for a hot pot meal by the time they reached Hyakumangoku Avenue. They found a restaurant that didn't look too expensive, and after they'd filled themselves up, were ready to enjoy a little more of the night air.

Go and Chigiri had never spent time like this together. They'd always eat and go directly to Go's hotel room, or at the most, leave the hotel for a meal and come right back as soon as they were finished. They were not so worried about being seen as they were anxious not to waste any time. They didn't believe they had the sort of relationship that had room for evening strolls.

They were satisfied by the meal and the sake, but back on the street, Go wanted a cup of coffee. It would have been easy to get one back at the hotel, but he wasn't in the mood for that, and asked Chigiri if there was a place that had good coffee. She knew of one shop back in Katamachi, so they walked all the way back there, but when they arrived, the corner she was sure the coffee shop had been on was occupied by a *robatayaki* barbecue. Thinking it might be a block in the other direction, they found a Kagayuzen shop with the shutters down. Her disorientation told Go how long it had been since Chigiri had enjoyed a night on the town. As for Chigiri, she had completely lost confidence in her ability to find her way around.

"Don't worry. I'm enjoying just walking. It's not that cold," Go reassured her. She refused to give up. The shop had been in business for so many years—it couldn't be gone. And eventually she did find it, the Peony Café. There was nothing special about it. Its age was apparent in the wooden door at the entrance. It was full of noisy young customers who had apparently come as part of an evening's activities that had begun with a typical end-of-the-year party. Go and Chigiri found a table in a quiet corner, and suddenly felt shy with each other.

"I haven't been here since I was a student," Chigiri said. "After that my lifestyle tended more towards noodles than coffee."

"Me, too. There used to be shops like this in Akasaka, but they're all gone now." They chatted about nothing in particular until it was almost ten. Go realized they'd only have an hour together at the hotel, but he was ready for it. The reasonable part of his brain told him the two of them ought to spend time like this, and he should see her straight back home to Tsurugi, but he had to admit that he wanted to make love to her. Chigiri finally made the decision for him. She looked at her watch, stood up, and announced that they'd better get back to the hotel.

Once they were alone, all they had to do was follow the flow of emotions that took them into a sexual world, but they both felt as though they had a mountain of things to say to each other. After kissing and embracing, Go was the one to begin.

"I don't really remember what I said that time, but paying a woman for a single act and then leaving her is not love. No matter how much you like her and are thankful for having met her, it's only a romantic sort of feeling, you can't call it love."

Chigiri was vaguely amused at his suddenly serious demeanor, but she listened just as seriously, deciding that she ought to properly understand what he was trying to say to her.

"When men want sex and are getting it, they begin to want to get more out of it, and start to have romantic feelings. They do it to soothe their consciences, to insist they are looking for more, and as kind of a prescription for pleasure. I don't know. Maybe women, too."

"I don't understand. Is it the same for women?"

"No, there are different kinds of women. Maybe some of them are like that."

"Wanting sex is not the same as love."

"I think dipping desire in a coating of romance makes it even better sometimes. On the other hand, completely ignoring such a feeling or trying to stamp it out can make sexual desire stronger. Sadism, masochism, is probably like that. There are probably some people who make you feel more romantic, and others that you want more just because of the lack of love. In either case, an emotion whose only purpose is to enhance sexual desire feels like romance, but it's not."

Chigiri began to blink her eyes and swallow hard, and then to sigh. These gestures indicated that she half understood what he was trying to say, but the heat of her building passion was getting in the way. On the one hand she was surprised that the comment she had made about the customer had affected him so strongly, but on the other she was dismayed that what she felt was no more than sexual desire because she wanted him to make love to her so badly.

"I'm sorry. I don't know where that came from." Go tried to cut off this line of thought, but he had made such a jumble of sexual desire, romance, love and sex, that he suddenly realized he'd spent his life thinking only about what was right in front of him: whether he wanted to make love to a woman or not, and if he did, how he'd do it, rather than taking an interest in anything else. He smiled wryly to himself.

He saw that Chigiri was at a loss, and knew that he should hold her to him, take off her clothes and send her to take a shower. But before he could do that, Chigiri seemed to have finally understood what he wanted to say. She looked him straight in the eye and asked, "Okay then, Go, what sort of feeling is love and romance to you?"

Go's entire body drank in those eyes, and now he was the one to blink and swallow hard. He thought for a few moments and finally responded,

"A feeling that something is missing."

"What?"

"When that person isn't around, when I'm not with her, I feel like I've lost something. That's love to me. No matter how passionate and furious the sex, unless I've got that feeling, I just fill up her absence with something else. That's not romantic. You can't call it that."

Go was describing a sensation he had never felt before. It wasn't until he met Chigiri that he was able to imagine "something missing." You could call him simple, and it certainly was a topic that poets have written about since the beginning of time, but it was new for Go. Comparing this new standard of his to all relationships he'd been in so far, including that time years ago when he first met his wife, he discovered he had never had the feeling he had now for Chigiri.

Go was terrified by this discovery, and he quickly added for the sake of Chigiri, who was having a hard time digesting his words, "It means that it makes me sad."

"Yes, I understand that."

"The person who ought to be there is not; that's why love can be sad."

Chigiri burst into tears. Now that he'd mentioned sadness out loud, she suddenly felt like she had permission to express her own.

Go Imai covered Chigiri's wet face in kisses. He held her to his breast and laid her on the bed. He wanted to make love then and there, and managed to get his pants off with one hand, but it wasn't until Chigiri too was half naked that he realized his organ would not become hard. He did his best to focus, but nothing changed: "My feelings have got my blood circulating throughout my body; I can't get it to concentrate down here where it usually is." Go was disappointed and deeply embarrassed. Chigiri continued to cry as if none of it mattered. The year was 1981. It was their last date of the year, the year they met again for the first time after twenty-five years.

9

When people are in love, they think about the meaning of love. When you're not in love, there is no reason to spend your time thinking about it. On the other hand, it's impossible even for someone who is in love to have a correct understanding of it.

Go Imai said that love was a feeling that something was missing and that it involved sadness. Not only was he explaining what love meant to him, but he was asking the person he loved to reciprocate that feeling. A person in love speaking about love will necessarily speak up for his own needs and demand something of the listener.

The term "lack of something" had a dramatic effect on Chigiri. She was forced to admit the gray-colored emptiness she felt when Go was away.

The New Year arrived and the permanent layer of winter snow was on the ground. The freezing wind blowing off the snow and the monotone scenery made her heart feel all the more vacant and lonely. Go had promised to visit in January, but he called the day he was to arrive saying stomach pain was preventing him from making the long trip. He was sure he had eaten pickled mackerel gone bad, and he would set another date soon. Chigiri glared at the phone receiver for its role in her misfortune as she set it back on the cradle. For the first time since they had met, Chigiri decided she wanted to go to Tokyo.

In her mind, Go was only himself when he arrived in Kanazawa or Tsurugi, and she hadn't wanted to imagine the man he might be in Tokyo. Since she succeeded in assuming it was a man in whom she was not interested, she had managed to get through the long days without him, but now that he had taught her about that lack of something, she wanted to go to Tokyo and see Akasaka first hand. She wanted to see Go making his way around the town. It might be a wonderful experience. On the other hand, it might be so disgusting she'd break out in hives just being around him, and lose all faith in their relationship.

But she wanted to go. She thought it might be easier if it was bad enough for her to want to give up on him. When he occasionally talked about his life in Tokyo, it sounded masochistic and had a chilling effect on her when what she needed was to cool down anyway. It might be helpful for her to see Go at his worst: vulgar and dirty.

"...I want to see you just like that."

"Ever since I got that food poisoning, it feels like my guts are rotting. I look and feel awful."

His stools were bloody; he was either constipated or getting the runs, but he still insisted it was after-effects of the blighted mackerel.

"So, you'll come?"

"I'll get some time off from Manraku and ask Matsuko to come help out for a while. My father isn't doing well either; we can't get him to eat." Kaho was in no imminent danger, but Chigiri knew it wouldn't be long before travel would be out of the question. Now was the time.

Chigiri had only been in the Tokyo area twice in her life. Once she went to Chiba for a week to stay with a friend from high school who was there for college. The other time was when Mayu was a toddler, and the two of them went to visit her ex-husband's sister in their Nakano apartment for two nights. The third time she made the trip it would be to see a man and have sex with him. Life was full of surprises.

"Tokyo winters are warm, aren't they? I was sweating in the subway."

"Why didn't you call like I asked? I was worried you were lost."

"I might get lost in Akadan, but not here. I knew exactly where I was going. The broadcasting station and the hotel built like a castle. Cities have lots of landmarks. Haven't you lost a little weight?"

"No, I've stopped drinking and that makes my beard grow a lot faster, that must be it."

"...I don't think so."

"I've missed you."

"I'm not sure I recognize you. Let me get a better look at your face. I guess it is you, Go. So this is your room and that's the phone you call from so late at night."

"And there's the poster. See? It is a car, and there are no naked women."

"Well, I'll be."

Go gestured triumphantly at the poster on the glass door between the living room and his bedroom. Chigiri put her bag down, but instead of sitting down on the sofa, she went over to the poster to inspect the girls in bikinis waving the checkered flag.

"But there are women on it."

"And they're wearing swimsuits, just like I said."

"I never said I thought they were naked."

"No, but that's what you were thinking. I could tell from your voice."

Go showed her into the bedroom and suppressed his desire to take her in his arms. He opened the door to the bathroom and indicated the pink toothbrush he had bought for her. He explained that he had thought of getting a hotel room, but he wanted her to stay here, in this unkempt room, with him.

"I'll refuse visitors while you're here, and there's no danger of my family showing up. Or would you rather take a trip somewhere?"

"It's not nearly as bad as you said it was; you weren't being honest with me!"

"You're here. That makes all the difference." Go went on to ask after her father. Chigiri explained that he spent more and more time asleep. The doctor had recommended oxygen, but Kaho just tore off the mask. She talked about Mayu, and how Matsuko had encouraged her to make the trip to Tokyo.

"I think she knows what's going on."

"I imagine she does. She probably had her share of problems with men as a young girl."

"You mean other than her divorce?"

"It's just intuition," concluded Go.

"I wouldn't know; my intuition doesn't work that way, I guess."

"She's family to you; you're too close to see it. Are you hungry?"

"I had a sandwich on the bullet train."

They talked about different things before getting to the subject of their minds and bodies. Go didn't want to think about his inability to perform the last time they'd been together in Kanazawa. He remembered it, but couldn't bring himself to mention it. He finally got the chance to embrace Chigiri when they had run out of topics.

"This is the smell," he murmured.

Chigiri started like a child who'd been caught being naughty.

"This is the smell I've missed."

"I was sweating in the subway."

The sunlight came through the windows on the west, and dyed their bodies amber. Go finally released Chigiri so she could shower. Afterwards she slipped her knit dress back on with nothing underneath. Go called his office on the floor above to say he didn't feel well and wouldn't be coming up that day. In truth, his stomach was feeling quite well, and thanks to the swirl of emotion inside it, he was full of energy. Go had changed his sheets and pillowcases that morning—it was one of the things he was good at taking care of.

Vowing to make up for his "problem" in Kanazawa, Go checked with the palm of his hand to see that Chigiri had nothing on under her dress, and then went directly into action. Last time, it was the deluge of words that had put the lid on their pleasure. Tonight they would have plenty of time for both.

The two took off their clothes and slipped in between the sheets, kissing for as long as their breath would hold out. After a while, Go asked to enter Chigiri from behind, and he lay down on his left side. The two, layered one on the other, were rolled up in the fetal position. Chigiri fit neatly inside Go's form.

"Wouldn't it feel good to be all rolled up like this, blown along by the wind?" he murmured softly into her ear, which was right below his lips.

"I wish we could take a nap out in the sun, just like this."

"Someday let's go find a wide open field and try."

"We'll catch cold."

Go's left arm was under Chigiri's left-hand side, and his hand fondled her right breast. His right arm, which was freer to settle on a place of its own choosing, was ensconced between her thighs. Every time his fingers moved, Chigiri tried to move out of their way and curled up even tighter. She was like a young fish twitching about trying to break out of its egg. She would be still and then convulse. She breathed out a deep sigh, and then released her voice. Once it was out, the bursts continued.

The two were rolled together, connected by Go's organ. For a while they didn't move. Go felt as though he was holding a warm cosmos in his arms. Chigiri, exploding with pleasure, felt like a cosmos firmly held in place by its axis.

In the end, they faced each other to make sure of each other's lips and chests and abdomens; they were able to endure the sweat and pulses and the waves of their urge for self-destruction. Curling up together like two babies in a womb became a special state for them. It meant they embraced the same air and moved around the same center, or desperately turned their blurred gazes in the common direction they were heading. A gondola with its upturned bow, a papaya with its fruit carved out—numerous images came to them, and went, but in the past, when the matter of the money had been between them, they had both had no choice but to face each other and search for what the other was feeling. Was it this time, or the last time they had met in Kanazawa—something had changed.

They went out for eel, and on the way back passed by a flower shop before buying a bunch of bananas at a fruit stand. Then they walked into a drug store. Akasaka drug stores were adorned with ads for energy drinks, and the shelves were piled high with them.

"Give me the best one you got," Go asked the shopkeeper.

"I'll have one, too," spoke up Chigiri.

They barely held their laughter in until they got back outside. They drank their purchases as they walked, and then stood them up on top of a stack of tabloid magazines outside a bookstore. The one they chose had two white breasts as large as domes on the cover, so they put their bottles on them so it looked like the domes were equipped with smokestacks.

"Do you always act like an idiot?" Chigiri asked.

"Always. For dozens of years."

Go kissed her as they walked. He didn't care if his staff caught sight of them. He felt flighty, even though he hadn't had a drink. He was in the mood to see just how mischievous he could act, and Chigiri was more than delighted to go along with anything he could come up with. Everything looked like it was up to no good; the people on the street, the signs on the bars, the purple sky, all of it, and it didn't bother her at all. It's probably me who has gone to ruin, she smiled to herself.

There were a few moments when she thought to herself how much more fun people had in Tokyo than she did in Tsurugi, and at those moments she would look down at her shoes. But in the next second, she'd lift her eyes and smile at Go walking next to her. When thoughts of Mayu's upcoming tests or the way her father looked sleeping with his mouth half open occurred to her, she shrugged her shoulders, shook her head, and took a deep breath to force them out.

They'd only had a little sake before dinner, but Chigiri was drunk on everything they did that evening. They went right to sleep and were awakened after nine by a call from work for Go. Chigiri showered and changed her clothes, but Go dragged her back to bed, saying he wanted to make love in the morning light. Chigiri pulled away saying she'd never done that before, but Go had his way. They both were soon naked again.

By the time they got around to eating at a local spaghetti place, it was a combination of breakfast and lunch. Afterwards, Go went up to his office on the sixth floor, and Chigiri went shopping in Akasaka-mitsuke, looking for a present for Mayu. Her daughter had been specific about what she wanted: a hair band covered in black cloth with white polka dots. If that wasn't available, she'd settle for the same pattern in plastic.

Chigiri would have to return to Tsurugi the next day and this was her only chance to shop. But her heart wasn't in it, and she couldn't find what she was looking for. She finally bought a muffler she thought would look good on Mayu and went straight back to the apartment. She dozed off until evening, thinking about Go upstairs at work. The phone rang twice, but she let it ring as she had been instructed. Chigiri believed him when he said he was the only one who was ever in the apartment. He had given her a key, but she couldn't sleep deeply, imagining someone coming down from the office or a member of his family appearing on the doorstep.

By the time she was fully conscious, though, the winter sun was already going down, and the sky was a dull, dark blue. She heard someone in the bathroom and the sound of a glass bottle rolling on the floor. It must be Go, she thought. He'd probably dropped the bottle of stomach medicine he kept in front of the mirror. She decided to pretend she was still asleep.

Coming out of the bathroom, Go aimed himself at the lump in the middle of the bed and threw himself on top of it, holding Chigiri tightly through the bedding.

"Get up, it's morning."

"Oh dear, I've got to be on my way!"

"Just kidding. It's still evening."

"You're awful! Does your stomach hurt?"

"What? So you were awake!"

"So?"

"I'm fine. I've gotten into the habit of taking that stuff, that's all. Let's talk about something else."

They went out to a hot pot restaurant, but they didn't laugh and weren't as silly as the night before. They weren't distracted by either the fruit shop or the drug store, and wordlessly went back to the apartment.

Chigiri sat down on the sofa, and Go pulled something out of a drawer in a chest in the corner of the room.

"Here it is," he said and handed it to her. It was a dagger. It was about ten inches long, a thin, almost perfectly straight dagger. It was the one Kaho had made so many years ago.

"So this is it," Chigiri responded, taking it in her hand. It was heavier than she expected. "My father fashioned the blade, and he always had the same workman in Kanazawa, a man who ran a wholesale *washi* shop, do the mounting, so this was probably the same. I don't think he made more than nine blades in his entire lifetime—and he gave them all away. We don't have a single one. Everything else he made were spades and pots and cooking knives."

"I'll have this returned to you after I die."

"What if I die first?"

"Then I'll make sure Mayu gets it."

"My father must have really liked you." She rubbed the black-lacquered sheath with a familiar hand. The dagger was less than an inch in width, and the blade just over five inches in length, and it shone coldly with the color of snow flowers. It was not clean, and the tip was slightly rusty. "I wonder if it can still cut? The tips of my father's blades were broad, and this one will probably shine if you get it sharpened. Do you mind if I use a piece of that scratch paper?"

Chigiri held a sheet of paper in one hand, and pulled the dagger straight down with the other. The paper cut cleanly in two. "The blade doesn't seem to be nicked."

"I brought it from home so I could look at it sometimes. It suits you better than it does me. Men look like idiots holding knives, but when women have them, they look alluring and dangerous."

"Now I'd like to cut something else."

"Cut up anything you like. The sofa and the curtains are all in tatters; I've got to start thinking about getting new wallpaper. There's nothing I'd regret losing. Cut up anything—but me and the phone line."

Chigiri's hand at that moment was driven by an impulse fraught with a touch of anger. Everything about this room and this place—Akasaka. It was all beautiful and exciting, and she would never have a connection to any of it. She hated all of the nights in his past—all the nights when Go, the man who lived here, was sloppy and irresponsible. He had told her she could cut it all to pieces.

It was a sad impulse that drove her, but she felt excited as she walked about the room searching for something to sacrifice to the dagger. She settled on the poster: the racing car and the two girls in bikinis waving the checkered flag. She held the tip of the blade at the top of the checkered flag. Then she described a circle around the neck and breasts of the girls. She drew it up to about their thighs, and made a tiny horizontal cut before pulling the blade straight down again. She had drawn the letter "G" on the poster without even touching the glass underneath.

"It's 'G' for Go, and it's ripped the girls in two. They deserve it."

"Now let me." Go took the knife from Chigiri and made similar motions. Now there was a small "C" inside the "G." "That's sort of how we looked last night." The two of them were still.

"This is me?" Chigiri asked.

"That's right. 'C' for Chigiri. We were attached right about here." It was a strange shape. The "C" was enveloped in the "G," and it looked a little bit like an ear. But at about the points where the blade was inserted, it looked like the letters were joined, the penis in the vagina.

Two arms reached around from behind Chigiri to hold her tight. Realizing he was still holding the dagger, Go quickly let go of her and put it down. Then he reached back to hold her again from behind, lifting her up and moving her to the bed.

The next day, Chigiri left for Tsurugi, taking a bullet train at about noon. Go was not there to see her off. For the next few weeks the poster with the mysterious ear-shaped cut in it remained on the glass partition. Go sipped his nightcap, gazing at the spot where the "G" and "C" connected.

So this is what it's all about. It really happens. All I can do is say the same thing over and over. I can't tell you things like this over the phone. I need to write a letter to explain in detail exactly what I mean, but even a master letter writer would have a hard time with this. And that's one of the things I discovered in my feelings for you. All I can say is that I "want" you, using a word that expresses physical desire.

I don't want to use worn-out words to express myself. Take "I love you," for example. People either use it to rationalize their sexual desires, or to awake in the other person a dead or dying emotion. Or it can be a term that you can't bring yourself to say. And by swallowing and not saying it, you end up fueling passion inside you until you can't bear it anymore.

So I can't use that either. I'll have to be more specific.

When I run my fingers across your nipples, it's not your nipples so much as your expression and your voice that I like. I like every part of you that has a protrusion: your nose and lips and fingers, your nipples and clitoris. And I love everything about you that is inverted. For example, the holes in your nose and ears, your navel, and of course all of your vagina. The sensation of each of those is concentrated somewhere inside you and it sends it out to each part of your body. That's the part of you I like best. I believe it's where you yourself are. I can imagine exactly where that spot is. You could say it was your soul or your heart, or your uterus, I guess. But I don't think so. I think it's a phantom place, a place I made and that I hold onto.

When I go to sleep at night, I'm in the habit of rolling up in a ball like I'm holding you inside me. I pretend my penis is deep inside you, and my index and middle fingers are quietly holding your clitoris. I can feel it with my whole body.

Then I explode in desire. It's only natural. But then I'm overcome with sadness that I can't fulfill it. I'm sad because your body is not here with me. Then I panic thinking about it all disappearing.

When I feel good, I can take those two fingers out of your clitoris and replace them with my penis and stimulate you until you come. But when I'm tired, I imagine us lying together rolled up, staying that way until we rot. That's kind of fun, too. I imagine the flesh falling off our bones and our hair blowing away. Does that sound disgusting?

But even then, I'd never say "I love you," those horrible words. The overcooked, dead-end words that everyone depends on. They're like an empty crucifix, a symbol, a code.

This is better than a code or words. Nobody else could ever imagine what it means.

At the end of the letter, Go Imai drew the symbol shaped like an ear, and sent it to Chigiri. Her reply arrived a week later.

> Dear Go, I feel you in every person I know who has ears. Whenever I see ears, something inside me gets excited. I want to go over to them and whisper something in those ears. Tokiyama and Nishimura have been telling me my eyes are shining recently. I tell them it's because I've seen someone with lovely ears.

I think I've learned a wonderful new word
that nobody will understand.

Dear C, My lovely, little, sensitive C.
Don't do anything dangerous. Don't get lost
in Akadan. That slender, wet fish that comes
leaping out of the dark water is mine. It belongs
to my index and middle fingers and nobody
else.

At the end of each of their letters, the writer included that mark that
would look like nothing more than an ear to anyone else.

When Go came to visit Chigiri the first week in March and in mid-
April, it was clear that Kaho had made it through the winter and his
disease was in remission. Mayu graduated from elementary school and
started junior high. Other than that, nothing of note was going on in the
Yamazaki household. Go, on the other hand, went home to his wife for
two days because he was dizzy and anemic and couldn't work. He was
reluctant to go see a doctor, but his son accused him of being egotistical
and his wife glared at him warningly. They were difficult days for him.

10

HISTORY TELLS US THAT Hakusan became an object of worship because the lives of the people living at the foot of the mountain depended on the water that flowed from it and the other surrounding peaks. Considering that the source of water for the five prefectures of Ishikawa, Toyama, Fukui, Gifu, and Aichi, was a white peak in the distance, it's quite likely that, even before the High Priest Taicho who sanctified the place, it had been worshipped by those who prayed for the peace and safety of the numerous populace.

Those ancient men of religion and fortunetellers must have worked in their respective villages and likely were granted much respect; however, according to the information passed on to us, Taicho, born at the end of the seventh or the beginning of the eighth century, was the first worshipper of Hakusan. From what we know, it would have been impossible for a high-ranking Buddhist priest like him to sneak off for a little mountain climbing. So, with the eyes of the masses on his every move, he started out with the smaller mountains in the vicinity, summiting Arashima and Iifuri, creating a route from which to approach Hakusan. It took him years to accomplish this, and, in the process, he garnered the respect and admiration of persons of culture who served as historical witnesses.

Stories concerning the first summits of Hakusan are recorded in *Hakusan, Ancient Stories of Peaks and Valleys* by Haruo Ishino. According to a story in it written by Hakuren Matsushita, a man who lived in the Heisenji area of Katsuyama City, the ascetic severity of mountain Buddhism was softened and refined because it was hidden behind the veil of feminine allure.

The story goes that when Taicho traveled through Katsuyama and into the mountains, he came to a flat place where he found a beautiful spring surrounded by cedars. As he meditated there, a heavenly maiden landed on a rock in the spring and explained to him that she was the goddess who lived at the top of Hakusan, and that this spring and its forest were her playground. She told Taicho that if he wanted to see her in her true form, he was welcome to visit her at the mountain peak.

This flat spot with the spring ultimately became the location of Heisenji Temple, the name meaning "flat springs." But going back to the goddess, if this was where she amused herself, one can be allowed an erotic fantasy or two. You can almost hear her seducing Taicho, enticing him to come to her up on the mountain.

Unfortunately, there is no record of the great priest discovering the goddess in her true form when he finally met her again at the summit. There are, however, lots of frightening stories of cats and snakes which lead one to believe that Taicho suffered greatly in his ensuing travels. Still, we are left with this one tale of how he met the beautiful goddess in this mysteriously beautiful setting, and know that it must have given him a few moments of bliss.

All of this, of course, is a lead back into the story of another man and woman who became drunk with bliss at this same location. In the late fall of Go Imai's forty-eighth year and Chigiri Yamazaki's forty-third, the couple revisited the Kimura estate and spent two days buried in the fiery color of maple leaves with which the grounds were covered.

Spring through fall of 1982 was for Go and Chigiri a time spent free of the matter of money. They no longer had to spend so much time and energy sizing each other up. Nor were they faced with the stone-cold wall that was to present itself later. It was a short time, but sweet and full of grace. Their second visit to the Kimura estate, the place where they had first been physically joined, would serve as a memory that would dye the rest of their lives vermilion.

A year-and-a-half before, during the fawn lily season when the estate was still cloaked in winter, there had only been a touch of the warmth of a fresh yellow-green. Now, deep in autumn, the placed was resurrected. The hills of the front garden appeared natural as the incline swept down to the pond covered in the leaves of the dozen maple trees. The colors ranged from blood red to golden yellow, shades of orange to flame red. Whether it was the variety of trees or the path of the cold air, the depth and range of color was evident on each tree and every branch.

Once inside the mansion, Go and Chigiri avoided the subject of Kaho. He was comatose, ready to bid this world good-bye at any moment. Fortuitously, he was free of the pain of his aged body. Matsuko came to Tsurugi to help out occasionally, and she had commented that she was certain that all of the sparks and metal he had breathed in over the years had lined his insides with iron, cauterizing his nerves.

Previously, he had had difficulty breathing because he kept tearing the oxygen tube from his nose and mouth and the nurse had to give him a shot to put him back to sleep. Now he did this less and less often, and he rarely spoke in a loud voice.

Chigiri's work at Manraku was going well, and her boss wanted her to come in every day. She was content, however, to make enough to pay her day-to-day expenses and preferred to spend as much time as possible at her father's bedside. During their visit to the Kimura mansion, Matsuko took her place at the hospital and Chigiri, in turn, prepared the meals for herself and Go. She went into the enormous kitchen, filled with trays and cooking utensils to feed large numbers of guests. Among the cooking memos Matsuko had left for them, Chigiri found a message from her: *Chigiri, autumn is a good time to turn up the heat!* Just as Go had assumed, Matsuko understood what was going on between the two of them.

Matsuko's instructions were precise and easy to follow. Dishes of pheasant meat and greens in season had already been prepared. All Chigiri had to do was boil the homemade soba noodles and their meal was ready.

They got the charcoal under the *irori* going, put the fish on to grill, and then sat knee to knee, passing a bottle of hot sake back and forth, refilling each other's cups; a fleeting moment spent as a married couple enjoying some time to themselves. They pulled the bedding out of the cupboard next to the *irori*, ignoring any danger of sparks flying out over them as they dozed, rolling over when their lips or noses got too hot.

"We might be dead of carbon monoxide poisoning by tomorrow morning," Chigiri mumbled.

"The ceiling's so high, I doubt that'll happen. It might be nice, though."

"What's nice?"

"I wouldn't mind dying here."

"You're a drunk."

"I'm drunk, but I'm not a drunk."

"Only drunks make distinctions like that."

"I've got proof. Here, look."

They had at some point assumed their ear-shaped position, but thanks to the bottle of sake they had drunk, it had a certain lack of precision and none of their usual urgency. But Go had had to call her attention to it, and at that moment as they both briefly considered the notion that this might be their only moment of happiness, with no more to look forward to in the future, they exceeded the boundaries of that happiness and began their slide into a hot hell of passion.

Chigiri reached ecstasy and Go ejaculated with their bodies connected. The shape of the ear had lost its shape, and they had rolled out of the bedding onto the tatami along with chopsticks that had somehow also gotten there. Go tried to pull away from Chigiri, who grabbed onto his backside to prevent him from doing so. He looked around for something, finally reaching out to grab the newspaper he had read before dinner. He carefully slid it under Chigiri so that when he pulled himself off of her, it caught the bit of semen that leaked out.

He got up and brought Chigiri's handbag over from the corner of the room. She pulled out some tissue paper, and told Go to look the other way while she cleaned herself up, giggling to herself. Go, with his thin back to her, lit a cigarette and asked what was so funny.

"You've dripped all over Ronald Reagan's face. And his wife's too, just a little. It does make me feel a little guilty," she said, sounding more exhilarated than sorry. The pleasure that had filled her body a few moments before had spilled over onto the American president, all the other countries in the world, and even into outer space. It melted over it all and slowly began sucking it all in. "We're alive, and that's why there's an American president, the Earth and the rest of the galaxy."

"What do you mean?"

"You know, as in 'I think, therefore I am.'"

"'Therefore I am,' huh?" Go didn't turn around until he'd finished his cigarette. His back laughed at Chigiri.

"I suppose I could say, 'I feel, therefore I am.'"

"So now you're a philosopher."

"Is that philosophy?"

"That's the sort of thing they say."

"Was it a male philosopher?"

"I'm pretty sure the 'I think' part was anyway."

"Maybe women feel rather than think."

"Did you feel something?"

"I'll be off to the bath." Go looked around to put out his cigarette, and Chigiri hurriedly stood up.

Before climbing into the tub, Chigiri washed herself, and as she did so, she wondered what it was like up there at the source of her spring. She pushed in the middle finger of her left hand to find out, and it felt as cool as if it were not her own skin and membrane. She pulled out her finger and brought it up to her nose; it was definitely not her smell. She put in her finger again to see once more what her own flesh felt like, and realized how good Go must feel when he was in there. It made her feel almost proud of herself. When she thought about her own genitals and how they felt, she thought the liquid that audaciously made its way in was about body temperature, and it felt good to her, too. She loved the little gift he'd left her; it was sweet in its helplessness.

Chigiri went back and forth; first she felt with her finger, then she felt with the flesh that the finger touched. It had recently exploded in delight, and the pleasure she felt had left something the pale color of a shard of shell inside. Realizing this she pulled her finger out again.

"Mind if I join you?" Go appeared suddenly, and Chigiri quickly doused herself with a bucket of hot water. The light falling from the naked bulb suddenly grew in scope because of Go.

"So! You've followed me here."

"Why don't we get in together?"

"I'm sure it's too late to turn you down." Chigiri plunked herself into the tub, and Go followed, grabbing hold of her from behind so they were back in their favorite position. Chigiri could feel something soft under her buttocks. It was a feeling she had missed. As a child, she had taken baths with her father. That something soft swayed in the hot water, and her father had never gotten angry even when she stepped on it.

"All good now," Go said.

"What is?"

The naked bulb turned the color of persimmon.

"It won't get hard for another two or three hours."

"Why is that supposed to be good?"

"It won't do to want to make love right away."

"So that's not why you're here in the bath with me?"

"You've got it wrong."

"Are you sure?"

"It doesn't bother you when I hold you like this, does it?"

"I don't want to stay in this hot water too long."

"Just a little more."

"Then tell me why it won't do to make love again."

"It's nothing. There's no problem."

"But you just said it's all good."

"It came out wrong."

"It sure did."

"I just want to hold you and look at you for a while."

"Really? But why?"

Chigiri turned around to look at him.

Beads of sweat stood out on his forehead. The bath was built as a protrusion from the rest of the house. It was run on propane gas, but there was an opening outside that had been used to add wood for a fire to heat the water. All four walls were made of the same wood as the tub, and it was all blackened with damp. The only thing glistening was the sweat on Go's forehead.

"Nothing, I just want to make sure."

"Of what?"

"I want to know why I like you even when I don't want to make love to you. What about you I'm so attached to. You know how men tend to get it all mixed together."

"You don't really *need* to untangle it."

"No, it's impossible."

"So give up."

"I know, but would you stand up for a second?"

Chigiri was already overheated from the bathwater. She got out and then sat down, in defiance of Go's request, on the drainboard and let out a sigh. She held both of her knees to her chest, and leaned against the bath, feeling its warmth through the wood.

"I'm boiled through. I don't think I can stand."

Go got out of the bath, brought over a little wooden stool and sat down on it right in front of her. They were close enough for their knees to touch. Go put out his hands to pull apart Chigiri's knees, and he looked her up and down, before letting his eyes settle in a lower spot. Then, as if searching for something he'd lost, they sped back up to her breast.

"I just don't know," he concluded.

"What don't you know?"

"Where in your body is it hidden—your special allure?"

"I'm not young anymore. There's nothing left to like. Not my breasts, not my tummy."

"Maybe it's your eyes."

"All I can tell you is that in thirty, forty years, it'll all be ashes. That's the only truth I can give you." Once she had said them, Chigiri was disturbed by her words. She might have been thinking of her father, or it might have been that she had a better look at Go under the light. His stomach seemed rounder than the top half of his body. He was not balanced, and must have looked more mortal.

"So is this going to be ashes?" Go took Chigiri's left breast in his right hand.

"Of course, it's nothing but fat. It will burst into flames as soon as I'm cremated, I'm sure." Go's hand made its way down to her stomach and then to the frizzly soft pubic hair, and spoke as he played with them.

"I guess this will burn, too?"

"It might be one of the last parts to go."

"I want it to last."

"On the other hand, if everything else went and only that remained, it would be embarrassing."

"Amazing."

"Uh huh," Chigiri responded, not really knowing what exactly was amazing.

"When you think of it, we were really going at it just a few minutes ago, and our bodies were linked together like that. But it will all be nothing but ashes. There won't be anyone around to remember it, either."

"Does that make you sad?"

"No, I'm impressed. It's only natural, but it seems like a miracle."

"I'll have to remember that."

Go went on. "We end up ashes, and it's as if none of this ever took place. It makes you think. There are people who were never involved in scandals or feuds, who never had children, and who nobody remembers. There must be millions of people buried in the past who thanked God for creating them, for letting them meet a certain person, for letting them fall in passionate love."

"You can't do much about two people dying and nobody remembering who they are, but what if one dies and the other person forgets the happy times they had together?"

"There are some people who need to forget to stay alive. But I'm not worried about us. And I wouldn't want to lead a life that requires having to forget what we've got."

"Ouch. Does that mean we're getting old?"

"Yes. I used to think there was nothing good about aging, but that's one good thing."

They both got back in the tub and discussed sex and death as if they had been alive for a hundred years. They washed each other, and were perfectly sober by the time they were through. Looking out of the window, they could see stars in the clear, black sky.

Go was worried about whether Chigiri would ever remember this night. At the same time, he knew he couldn't do anything about it if she didn't. Chigiri, on the other hand, was confident she'd remember this night until her brain was incapable of processing any form of thought. The only thing she was unsure of was whether she'd remember what had happened on which of the two nights they were together.

As she had foreseen, the second night was similar to the first, except that Chigiri cried after they had sex the second night. It was something

Go said.

"This sort of passion can't last."

Chigiri cried because she agreed with the words, but they made her angry. She knew he was right, but wanted to argue. Every possible emotion came to the fore, spilling out as tears. But afterwards, she mumbled once in a timid voice, "That's why we feel it so."

All life ends in death. This is the first rule of fate. The second rule is that life strives desperately to continue despite the fact that death is a given. Chigiri's father, Kaho, was an excellent example of these two rules fighting it out. Kaho had been lent the battleground of his body and he watched from the sidelines, occasionally sighing, waiting to see which side would win. His face no longer expressed joy or pain.

One day at the end of December, his breathing became ragged. He began to need phlegm removed from his throat several times a day, and as the days wore on, this increased to once every two hours or so. His face began to change. The red complexion from years of sake and fire turned dark and became shriveled. His tongue, which occasionally peeked out from between his lips, turned the color of dead leaves.

So this is the death mask, observed Chigiri calmly, as she gently rocked Kaho through a moment of apparent discomfort.

During the New Year's holidays, she and Mayu took turns staying with Kaho all night, and she asked Tokiyama to give her some time off at Manraku. After Mayu went back to school, Chigiri asked Matsuko to come help. Kaho held on for a week after the doctor declared it would be a matter of a day or two, but early one day in mid-January, during the weekend, while Mayu was with him, he quietly breathed his last.

She awoke to the unnatural quiet, and by that time it was too late for the usual camphor injection or a heart massage. Her grandfather was gone and the nurses made no attempt at extraordinary measures. Chigiri reassured her that this was all for the better, but Mayu cried bitter tears for her perceived inattentiveness.

When people die, huge chunks of sadness come barreling down on their loved ones. They hurt when they hit, but if you try to avoid them, you'll eventually be crushed by even larger and heavier chunks. All you can do is turn one cheek, then the other, and repeat until the flow has stopped or at least slowed.

Kaho died at the ripe old age of eighty-six. His aging body had been ravaged by so many illnesses and symptoms that even the doctors couldn't keep up with them. Chigiri and Mayu were devastated by the loss, but they did feel relief that it was all over.

The winter that year was warm. On the day of Kaho's simple funeral held at the Yamazaki home, the white camellias and narcissus made their stately appearance, shining as brightly as the top layer of snow, just beginning to melt in the winter sun.

Snow, flowers, and purifying light. Amidst all this white, Chigiri came home from the crematory bearing the bones of Kaho wrapped in an urn covered with white cloth. The funeral was attended by their few relatives, Tokiyama from Manraku, and Mayu's friends from school. The atmosphere was not so much filled with the darkness of death as it was with the resiliency of human beings playing out the ceremonies required of a funeral, and a few of the mourners were moved to a smile or two in the midst of it all. There was also a joyful anticipation that they might have an early spring.

They all went home, however, and the pleasant weather did not last. A moist and heavy snow fell, and Kaho's urn adorned the tiny family altar. Since the family had not had much of a New Year's celebration, Matsuko came by with a bag of *mochi*. Chigiri sautéed it in a frying pan and added a little sugar and soy sauce to put on the altar in front of the urn. Then, for the first time in a while, she had a good cry.

Go arrived in mid-February to burn incense and pay his respects after all of the accompanying ceremonies were over and people were no longer making frequent visits. Chigiri understood that he was trying to avoid a time when she would be preoccupied, and did not mistake his distance for a lack of interest. Indeed, they spoke on the phone often, but she was a little nervous about his arrival sending her into a different world entirely.

He showed up on a Monday afternoon while Mayu was at school. He was wearing the same trenchcoat he had worn almost exactly two years earlier when he had come back looking for the Rokuro Cedar. Chigiri was astonished to see that his face looked so much thinner, making his eyes and nose larger, and his eyebrows thicker. In the two months since they'd seen each other, Chigiri had been through quite a bit, but there had also been something happening with Go, and it definitely was not good. Nor was it over.

While Go offered incense at the altar, Chigiri watched him from behind, wondering what could be the matter. As soon as she caught her imagination entering a certain realm, however, she firmly shut the door on it.

Go, still facing the altar, put his hands together in a position of prayer, but he could feel Chigiri's eyes on him. He had indeed had his own reasons for waiting so long before he made the trip to Tsurugi. On the twentieth of December, he had woken up after a year-end party with terrible stomach pain. He finally went to see a doctor who put him into the hospital for a week of tests. He made it home for the holidays, returning to the doctor a few days later for the diagnosis he had known was coming and which he had spent the past year readying himself to accept.

A young doctor from the teaching hospital explained that he had a malignant rectal tumor, and encouraged him to immediately schedule surgery to remove it.

Go had grimaced and said that he wouldn't mind so much if it were in his stomach, but a rectal tumor would mean removing everything from his rectum to his anus, and then being fit with an artificial excretory device. How, he wondered, would he manage to have sex with Chigiri? Would they be able to achieve their favorite ear-shaped position?

What he told the doctor was that he'd just as soon pass on life if it meant having to give up women. It was not a nice way of putting it, but it was the truth. The doctor refused to give up, encouraging him to go home and discuss the matter with his wife and children. Go asked if the surgery would cure him of the disease, and the response was, no, it had progressed too far, and the surgery would only extend his life a little longer, but wouldn't that time be important to him?

Following this discussion came one at home that lasted much longer. Go stuck with his decision not to have the operation, and asked the doctor for any other form of treatment that might be available.

He took medicine that stopped the diarrhea and internal bleeding, but it ruined his appetite. He kept up with his work and continued to consume alcohol. He still spent most of his time at his apartment in Akasaka, but his staff kept an eye on his obviously failing health and made sure he didn't overdo either.

Go was not nearly as philosophical about the whole matter as he appeared to be. Nor was he acting as reckless as his family accused him of being. He wanted badly to continue to live. But the tumor was less than two inches from his anus, and no matter how well the surgery went, he'd still have difficulty with both sex and urinating, and he couldn't bring himself to go through with it.

He almost felt it would be easier if the disease had progressed far enough to make the procedure meaningless, relieving him of the need to make a decision. It was apparently not a sudden-onset sort of disease, but the result of long years of a selfish, irregular lifestyle. He realized that the two years he had had with Chigiri had been like a divine gift, a going-away present from the gods. This notion helped him make his mind up.

"It must have been hard for you," Go said to Chigiri, turning back towards her.

"From the looks of you, you've had hard times of your own." Chigiri got up the courage to voice her observations, and Go nodded obediently.

"It looks like I won't be around for as long as Kaho."

Gloom invaded Chigiri and settled inside of her.

"So you have been ill. Have you seen a doctor?"

"Don't worry, I can still make love to you." Go smiled through reddening eyes.

"Have some tea."

"Not here in front of your father."

"What are you thinking?"

"Is the front door locked?"

As before, they went into Chigiri's room. She had already had a bath in the reheated bathwater from the night before. She turned the kerosene heater up high and pulled the curtains shut. They held each other fiercely. Go's mouth smelled of breath mints, and Chigiri's of dried persimmon. Go tried to guess how many more times he'd be able to make love to her, and went slowly through the motions of foreplay until a musky smell rose like a film from Chigiri's lower body. The bed frame squeaked and groaned, so they stopped moving, afraid someone might hear. It was a perfectly quiet afternoon.

White fragments began falling inside Chigiri's head. They weren't camellia petals, or pumice stone, or Kaho's ashes. The fragments were a sign that a whirlpool was coming to swallow her. *More slowly,* she whispered into Go's ear. *Please.*

Despite her own plea, Chigiri charged headlong into the whirlpool.

Chigiri drove Go to Kanazawa for the evening train back to Tokyo. On the way they stopped at the Rokuro Cedar in Hinomiko, and parked the car by the side of the road. The sun from the west came pouring through the bare branches, and a cinnabar-colored mosaic was cast into their faces, rendering them stock still in its brilliance.

The dead leaves from the labyrinth of branches spread out across the ground had been drenched in the snow and turned black. On top of that was hardened snow like a layer of ice, and from underneath it poked the butterbar sprouts of early spring.

Here, too, was the dappled cinnabar light, swaying gently—both light and shadow, in the gentle wind.

They drew near to the great branches crawling over the ground, and Chigiri's foot sank in the soft bed of dead leaves. Go took her hand and managed to make it to the center of some branches separated by a few strides. Cedars are evergreens, and there were of course patches of gray leaves on the branches. Go wondered if it had shed so much foliage due to its age.

There was only one flat, comfortable place to sit. Go threw one leg over to straddle it, and Chigiri followed suit, sitting in front of him, facing in the same direction. Directly in front of them was a single straight branch; it seemed to be the highest point on the tree. Looking up to the top, they instinctively closed their eyes when scraps of leaves blown by a breeze came fluttering down, at first like sunlight diced up by the overlapping layers of leaves and falling in pieces. Go put his arms around Chigiri, who leaned back into him and closed her eyes. She could see the movement of light and shadows through her eyelids.

"Go, are you going to die?" she asked with her head resting on his shoulder.

"That's what I've been told."

"When?"

"I don't know yet, but I'll let you know when it happens."

"How?"

"I'll send you a message only you can understand."

"Can't you live some more?"

"I don't think so, but I'll come back here after I die. Don't ask for anymore than that."

"I'm going to die, too."

"Someday. Sooner or later."

"After you die, we'll come back and sit here. Just like this."

"I wonder if I'll be able to hold you." Go held Chigiri's back and stomach in his arms. It was their usual position.

"Will you hold me even when you're an invisible spirit?"

"I want to."

There were no houses; nothing but the stumps of rice in all four directions. The wind brought them the far-off sound of a train. There in the middle of the field among the accommodating roots of the Rokuro Cedar, Go and Chigiri sat impervious to the cold, layered together like two flower petals, watching the sun go down.

The surface of the branch where they sat, as well as the thick one growing straight up, revealed patches where the bark had been peeled off. They didn't know what had happened, but they imagined that the Rukoro Cedar had seen its share of difficult times. Wind and water—maybe even fire. Go supposed that it would continue to live on, while Chigiri realized that it had aged greatly from when she was a child, and wondered what she would do if it died. She pulled Go's arms around her more tightly.

Chigiri had finally accepted the notion of her father's death, and was unable to imagine losing Go. She didn't want to think of anything other than the present, savoring every moment.

Go missed his train, but got a seat on the next one. The memory, in both of their minds, was dyed in the soothing light, both transparent and dappled, that covered them. Go took it as a form of advance consolation for the changes his body was about to make. Chigiri accepted it as the smile of her father, who was already as high up as the sun.

11

It was written that the name Tsurugi came from swords and not from cranes. Anything that shines is precious: this is a notion of beauty that is the same anywhere and in all ages. Gold is a color that evokes images of modern happiness and profit that contrasts with the shine of silver, linked to a more sacred mentality. The reason swords have so often been entrusted to shrines is probably because gods are believed to reside in anything that shines. It's interesting to note that a *tsurugi*, or sword, originally referred to the broad, symmetrical weapon such as the one held in the right hand of the Buddhist guardian deity Fudomyo'o, whereas a *katana*, or Japanese sword, is the proper term for that *tsurugi* sliced vertically in half. Divinity may reside in them, but they are also weapons, to be used against men. To improve their cutting edge, they are sharpened so that they shine, and so the best blades are divine and lethal both—not a contradiction, as deities kill quite often and are thereby feared.

Perhaps this notion shares something with worshipping the silver-white summit of Hakusan, and indeed, in that mood, any shiny surface, be it snow or the water's surface, begins to look pure and sacred.

Beneath the snow is black dirt. Riverbeds are covered in slimy moss. Even Hakusan looks better when viewed from far away. The blade of a holy sword is made of a valuable raw steel. The name means "treasured steel," but it is made with clumps of a dull, gray color. That dull color is only evident when the raw steel is first made. Months and years turn it into a rusty color, and it can look completely worthless. To swordmakers, however, such a metal is valuable enough to lock up in the vault of a bank. The metal is made over several days, smelting a large amount of sand iron, heating and blowing air on it using foot-operated bellows. The result is a small amount of iron clumps, and within those clumps is an even smaller amount of the precious raw steel.

In modern days, we get the feeling that this metal might surely be more quickly produced in a smelter, but the trick to producing it is blowing it with bellows at a low temperature. This is the only way to make "treasured steel." Production has ground to a halt these days.

Let us for now, though, set aside the problems of producing raw steel, and return to our story. After Kaho's death, a lump of "treasured steel," small enough to fit in the palm of a hand, was found in a drawer of the Yamazaki family altar. On the paper it was wrapped in was written in Kaho's hand, "For Hisahiko Ishida, Togi blacksmith."

Chigiri told Go about it during a phone call after he was back in Tokyo. Go said that he remembered seeing that piece of raw steel. While they were filming the documentary, Kaho had brought it out to show them so they could learn the basics of swordmaking. It looked like nothing more than a clump of scrap iron from which a few air bubbles had escaped. Go had remembered it because of what Kaho had told them. He said that it had the "unbending, unbreakable" property required of a sword, a property that was usually considered an oxymoron. Steel that doesn't break will bend; if it doesn't bend, it will break. The "treasured steel" was the only steel that could achieve this apparent contradiction.

"He must have believed that even if he usually made plows and shovels, he'd be able to make another blade someday as long as he had that piece of metal." Go's comment was based on his own imaginings, but Chigiri didn't believe her father had retained such aspirations. She was pretty sure he had made his few daggers many years before, during his thirties and forties.

Swords and daggers were basically the same except for their size. Blades for swords had holes in them to attach the hilt, and only blades with these holes were considered dangerous weapons and in violation of the Firearm and Sword Control Law. A dagger without holes was categorized as a "pocket knife."

In the old days there were a number of swordsmiths who had given up their trade to become blacksmiths, and they too had made the occasional dagger to keep in practice. These days, however, with the lack of "treasured steel" and the decline in craftsmen, even daggers had become a rarity. Kaho must have written "For Hisahiko Ishida, Togi blacksmith" dozens of years before. Chigiri wasn't sure who the man was or where he could be found. Go suggested looking him up in the phone book.

Before speaking to Go about it, Chigiri had planned to leave the steel where she'd found it. Now, though, as she replaced the receiver, she thought that she'd respect her father's will of who-knew-how-many years ago as well as the existence of this clump of steel by finding this Ishida and hoping that he might see it made into a blade.

She found an Ishida family in the town of Togi, and the man named Hisahiko had a younger voice than she'd imagined. He told her over the phone that, as a boy, he remembered going with his father to the Yamazaki Sword Shop on the main street of Tsurugi.

Hisahiko said, "I think we're probably related. There was some kind of connection a long time ago."

There was a swordsmith named Tomoshige Fujishima, Hisahiko

continued, who came to Tsurugi from Echizen. During the Ikko Uprising of Buddhist zealots, he escaped to Etchu. One of the families in his group eventually went back to Tsurugi, and another went to Togi on the Noto Peninsula. The latter were the Ishida ancestors.

"That's interesting. How long ago was that?"

"About five hundred years ago." He sounded so serious that Chigiri was unable to laugh. Instead she responded just as seriously:

"I don't know if my father ever told me the whole story, but he always insisted that Tomoshige Fujishima was an ancestor of ours."

"That's what my father always said, too, so it must be true."

"I never paid attention, but I should have believed him. His last few years he was so delusional."

"My father died when I was seventeen. It wasn't a delusion, just a matter of history."

Chigiri still wasn't sure what to think, but she went on to tell him about the lump of metal she'd found with his name on it. Hisahiko was a farmer-cum-blacksmith. He had never seen raw steel, and hesitatingly but eagerly said he was anxious to get a look at it.

Both Go and Chigiri were certain that this would be his final trip. They were also determined that in the instant before each of them died they would look back and realize that this had been the night they had released the brightest and strongest light, and that all the days afterwards would be devoid of meaning in comparison. With this in mind, Chigiri decided that she'd better not spend it looking glum. She gripped the steering wheel of her car, and looked casually out at the scenery along Route 249. She rolled her head and spoke as if the whole business was inconsequential.

"I suppose it makes sense that we've got relatives from five hundred years ago in Togi. Even the names of the places are similar.

"Tsurugi means 'cranes come,' Togi means 'wealth comes.' They're both lucky names," said Go in the passenger seat, looking as though he was trying to lift himself higher. His weight was almost half of what it had been when they'd met in Tsurugi a little more than two years before.

"And not only that, 'tsurugi' really came from 'blade,' and 'togi' could actually be the verb for 'sharpen.' We've got to be related."

"It depends on how you look at those five hundred years. It's a pretty big block of time. But it's only ten times as long as my life, so it doesn't seem that far away, does it?"

"How many days would you have to mark off a calendar for five hundred years to pass? You could calculate that. It's not that long if you can actually count it out. If you put our ages together, it would only be five times as long."

An awareness of the limited time we humans have on earth is usually accompanied by the feeling of immortality that accompanies a grasp of some universal truth. Accordingly, if, at that moment, the road running beneath Go and Chigiri had sent them flying off into the spring sky, neither of them would have said a word and merely smiled.

Neither of them wanted to be bothered with the small-minded matters of the present. Go felt like an pure-minded philosopher and Chigiri had turned into a child from whom words might suddenly flow as ceaselessly as the sound of the waves they were drawing closer to.

From the moment they turned onto the Chirihama Driveway, the two of them had been filled with a magical surge of cheerfulness and vigor. As they drove north along the sea, about the time they reached Oshima Beach, they had to open the windows and let in the cold air to cool themselves down.

They had a hard time finding the home of Hisahiko Ishida, but they chatted about the fun of concluding five hundred years of separation, and enjoyed the search.

In early April, the Noto Peninsula, and in particular the town of Togi, was a brilliant sight to see, but it was also beset by a cold, dry wind. By the time they arrived at the Ishida home, Go felt like a plate of dried-out *mochi*, but he followed Chigiri, although at a much slower gait, up to the front door.

On the other side of the irrigation ditch was a main house with another building attached to it. Across it was a small hut surrounded by galvanized sheet iron with a chimney sticking out of one of the walls. Chigiri noticed two welding tanks outside the hut, and knew it was the blacksmith workshop. Instead of knocking on the front door, she went over to the open hut to peek inside. There wasn't a sign of anyone having been there recently. The fire was cold, and pliers and hammers for grasping and beating the heated metal were covered in a layer of brown dust, as were pieces of iron of various shapes and sizes. Chigiri, clad in a dress of a soft fabric, looked around fondly. Her eyes shone as she looked at a strangely shaped tool with long, curved finger-shaped clutches.

"We had one of those in Tsurugi when I was a child," she said, explaining that it was used to collect clumps of wakame seaweed. There were flat hoes, three-pronged forks, and hatchets, and prices were displayed on a sign under the title of "Prices Set by the Togi Blacksmiths Cooperative." That had to mean there were other shops nearby.

Chigiri took a deep breath of the iron-filled air, knowing for sure that the people in this town must be related to her. By and by a man appeared at the door to the hut. He was over forty, a small man with a round face.

"Forgive me for just barging in," Chigiri said, as she and Go scurried back outside. "I thought for a moment that my father must be in here; I was drawn in, I guess."

She got the feeling that Hisahiko Ishida looked like her father in his younger years, but he had never had such a gentle smile. When she was finally finished apologizing, she somewhat bashfully introduced Go as the TV producer who had made the documentary on Kaho.

Between the hut and the front door to the house were a white magnolia in bloom and a huge black persimmon tree. Chigiri recognized the species because there had been one in the garden of the house she had been brought up in, the one she'd lived in before her family had retreated to Chimori. Her father had taught her that it was used for the mounting of daggers because of the beautiful pattern created by its striations. It was as valuable as mulberry or ebony.

"A black persimmon." Chigiri stood looking up at it. It was still bare of leaves, and Hisahiko Ishida was apparently unaware of its name. "It was used for the handles of daggers. We had one, too."

"That tree has always been here. It must have been planted generations ago. All jokes aside, it certainly seems as though we must have the same bloodline."

"Were you joking when I talked to you before?" Chigiri goaded him playfully.

The conversation quickly warmed as Hisahiko led them into the main house, and his wife, a woman with a thick neck and broad shoulders, served them tea. The life they led dictated farming in the summer and blacksmithing in the winter; it couldn't be an easy one. Both Hisahiko and his wife had a healthy, ruddy complexion that made Go's ash-colored face look even darker and more hollow as he sat at the electric foot warmer still set up in the middle of the room.

Chigiri pulled the lump of "treasured steel" from a paper bag and set it on the table over the foot warmer. Hisahiko picked up the unimpressive lump and looked it over.

"A man who sells steel tells me it's worth quite a bit. Thank you very much." He bowed and appeared at a loss about how to proceed. "Mr. Imai, er, do you still work in television?"

Hisahiko's attempt to place Go in this scenario had not a hint of acrimony or evil intent to it, and Go and Chigiri had set off on their errand with the notion that they would be ready for even uncomfortable questions about their relationship. It might have been the magic of a five-hundred-year history, but they felt as though they would be accepted here.

"Yes, I've been working to get by, but I'm closing up shop when I get back to Tokyo." Go seemed relaxed and unperturbed. This alone communicated his relationship with Chigiri to Hisahiko. "I've been ill, and I'm afraid this is going to be my last trip out here," he said more to Chigiri.

"If that's the case," spoke up Hisahiko, "how about staying at a small country inn my eldest sister and her husband keep in a place called Noto-machi? You keep heading down the Noto Peninsula and over towards the Toyama Harbor side and past Anamizu, closer to the tip of the peninsula. It won't take long by car. Noto has stark, cold images, but the ocean spreads out to the south and you can see the Tateyama Range across the bay. I can't just take this steel without giving you something in return. As you can see, we don't have much, so let me do this. I'll give my sister a call. I'll tell her we've got family from five hundred years ago. You haven't lived until you've tried her *hine* sushi. You'll find it easy to get around here because there are no mountains..."

And so Hisahiko accepted them and sent them on under his gentle gaze. Even the road was accepting of them as they sped off in Chigiri's tiny car. It wasn't long before the simple map Hisahiko had drawn brought them to their destination, an inn called Tonami. At the top of a hill with an undisturbed view of Toyama Harbor was what looked like a large kitchen garden. From there, they approached a wood and white-walled structure that looked more like an old-fashioned farm house, to find it was indeed the inn.

They couldn't see as far as Tateyama, but they got a vague glimpse of the city on the other side of the bay. Go wondered if it might be Toyama or Takaoka, but Chigiri was sure it was Toyama. She was vehement that this was the case, and the sheer strength of her emotion told Go that she was suppressing some other emotion. As the sunset turned the sky violet and the sea in front of them disappeared, so did the playfulness they had enjoyed that afternoon.

This was it; their final night together.

The months and years that made up five centuries—they could be counted but not personally confirmed. What they had now was make-believe sake with the magic spell broken. They could no longer pretend to drink it or pretend to be drunk on it. They had a limited amount of time left, and the reality of it had struck them. The few minutes they spent looking at the ocean were moments stolen from that precious time.

The couple who kept the inn were waiting for them. If the wife was Hisahiko's elder sister, Chigiri thought, she too would be a relative of some sort. She looked at the woman, who appeared to be in her mid-fifties, hopefully, as if searching for a clue that would help her get through this night.

"We only have three guest rooms, and there are no reservations for tonight, so relax and enjoy yourselves. The stone bath is heated."

Her husband had on a cardigan, but she was dressed in a kimono and sleeved apron, her split-toed socks were ironed and neat.

The rooms were more luxurious than they had expected. Compared to the Kimura estate near Heisenji, it didn't seem as empty and unused. It was the sort of comfortable place you could enjoy while traveling because it was so strange to ordinary life. There was sparkle in the flowers in the tokonoma, the zelkova table, and the fluffed cushions. It seemed like a luxurious hotel, known only to the very few wealthy customers it deigned to cater to. The very thought filled Chigiri with embarrassment when she thought of the casual way Hisahiko had offered to put them up. She wondered what he had told his sister. The innkeepers were certainly treating them as a middle-aged couple who needed a discreet place to stay. They were attentive, but said no more than necessary.

"As soon as my brother called, I sent out for shrimp and fresh fish, but I'm afraid it will be a while until dinner is ready."

"Thanks for taking us in on the spur of the moment. We'll take a bath and settle in. Would you mind giving us a bottle of beer first?" Go's voice was clear and did not sound tired. The woman indicated that she would comply and got up to leave.

"Oh, and one more thing," Go added as she was about to leave, "I'd like some good sake served cold. A sake so good that I wouldn't mind dying after drinking it." The woman smiled and nodded, and mentioned two or three brands. Go chose one, but Chigiri already felt drunk. Her eyes swam and her heart beat loudly in a sense of panic. All she could do was sit there looking out at the ocean.

The woman left, and Go left Chigiri to take a bath. She did her best to suppress the emotion that was quickly overtaking her. She knew the feeling would come back to overwhelm her hundreds or even thousands of more times, but she wanted to somehow not let it get the better of her that night. To turn this night into a vivid, shining memory she had to somehow cut off this feeling that was dragging her further and further down, below the earth. It was more like the pain of having part of her body severed than it was sadness. She knew it would be back to haunt her endlessly until the day she died. Tonight was her last chance to chisel the brilliance of Chigiri Yamazaki into Go's memory. When it came time for him to leave this world, and he unwound the last thin layer of cloth that represented his consciousness, she wanted to make sure she was sewn into the last shred of it, and she wanted to be beautiful for him.

While Chigiri was in their room fretting, Go was in the bath—one carved out of a large stone. He enjoyed the scratchy feel of it on his back, and patted the abnormal swelling in his stomach. Rather than a lump, it was a living being, almost like a pet he was keeping. It didn't hurt at all, and this was one of the reasons why it didn't seem like a part of his body. According to the doctor, instead of reaching his spinal cord, the cancer spread out from the peritoneum to part of his small intestine so that, while threatening his liver, it steered clear of his biliary tract, sparing him the worst pain. The only problem was that he could only eat and drink in small amounts if he wanted to avoid half a day of excruciating indigestion.

Go hadn't invited Chigiri into the bath with him because he hadn't wanted her to see him naked, looking like a frog with a swollen belly. He had thought about how he would approach her, but hadn't had any good ideas. Unsure whether he would even be able to make love to her, Go sat for a while in the bath listening to the water drip, and finally made up his mind.

All things had a beginning and an end, he realized. Days moved from one to the next because the Earth spun on its axis. If you looked at it as cosmic scenery, it was nothing more than endless repetition. But this was the last such one he could spend with Chigiri.

What was true for this bath made of rock was the same for the dagger Kaho had made, and the lavender dress Chigiri was wearing. They would continue to exist after he was dead. Someone else might touch Chigiri's body, he realized, astounded at his childish jealousy. Since he'd met her, he'd experienced the reality of how simple and infantile one became after falling in love. Even now he was in awe at the power of simple romance; how it had nudged him out of the complicated weave of intellectual and rational society. He wondered if humans might have developed intellect and reason as a way to harness the power of romance and love. If that was the case, it was impossible to further analyze or break down one heart that loved another, it was an organic bond that could not be deciphered. To put it more simply, it was the heart in its original form, singular but strong.

Trying to figure out why you loved someone was pointless. You might be able to explain why you *dis*liked someone, but there was no good reason for falling in love other than that an aphrodisiac had been sprinkled down from heaven.

The more he thought, the less confused Go became. He'd make Chigiri burn with passion this evening. Nothing else was needed. If his organ refused to function properly, he'd use every other method he could think of. In fact, why else was his head placed at the top of his body?

His decision made, he was almost childish in his utter determination. It had not begun, however, with sexual desire. It was the result of an entanglement of feelings unmotivated by the ecstasy he would achieve through the act of ejaculation. His entire being was filled with the desire to be buried inside Chigiri's body. Even if she couldn't continue feeling it forever, he wanted to leave behind the pleasure of their sex, something she could look back on and remember. He gripped the member that maintained its shape but floated softly in the hot water.

Dinner that night at Tonami was skillfully prepared and delicious, which only made Go more despondent over his inability to enjoy it. Chigiri used a visit to the kitchen to ask for more sake as a pretext to explain to the woman who brought them tray after tray of food that Go was ill and couldn't eat much, and she hoped they would not be offended by what was left on the plate.

"I see," the woman replied. "I'll put out smaller servings, then."

"The grilled fish was delicious, and the sakura tofu, too. I'm really sorry about the food, and, as you can see, drinking is no problem."

As soon as they were finished eating, the woman came to lay out their bedding. Chigiri didn't know if it was because she had heard Go was ill, or whether they always did it this way, but she was grateful Go would be able to lie down.

Neither Go nor Chigiri hurried because they knew this would be the last time they would make love. Chirigi took her time in the bath. She removed her make-up and cooled down her reddened skin with lotion. She took so long, in fact, that Go finally called her back in.

Chigiri took off her wrap and was dressed only in a thin lace slip that showed her breasts and the dark area below her waist. She had bought it just for the occasion. It was sheared beneath her nipples, and the front hem had a deep slit in it. She wasn't young anymore, but she knew it made her look sufficiently sexy.

For a few moments, Go merely gazed up at Chigiri in her glowing charm, and then pulled the hem of the slip so he could put both of his arms around her. He was set on fire by her youthfulness, and at the same time was struck by a dull pain.

They lay down on their sides and looked at each other, and kissed. Go took off his wrap and covered their bodies with a blanket. He was naked, but Chigiri was like a butterfly still wrapped in a white cocoon.

Go turned her over so they could take their ear-shaped position and he could hold her lower body with his hands. Chigiri curled up like a fetus, and Go took the same form, fitting himself tightly against her back. Chigiri couldn't see the lump in his stomach this way.

Go's arms wrapped themselves around Chigiri. His right arm, the freer of the two, slowly rubbing her breasts and stimulating her down below. When he heard her breath grow ragged his fingers stopped and moved to her stomach and sides. It was as if he was afraid of her running straight into ecstasy, and wanted her to slow down. Then he went back to work until she began to dash off again, and once more made her wait a while longer.

When Go put his fingers through the holes in the lace to touch her nipples, Chigiri could not keep her voice down. She didn't want to cry out because she was sure her voice would carry off the feeling before she could dye her entire being in it. She held her breath and tried to suppress her pleasure, holding it inside, filling up a jug somewhere deep inside of herself. All it took, though, was a movement of Go's fingers to agitate the water and splash some of it out, over the edge. At those times, she let out her voice just a little and let a smidgeon of her feeling escape. At the sound of her voice, Go's organ gained new power, and he was ready to penetrate her at any moment.

But he didn't. And Chigiri didn't want him to. They wanted to stretch out each second, making it last as long as they could.

Chigiri's slip was covered in sweat and clung to her skin. Whenever it moved over her nipples tight from the stimulation of Go's fingers, it was like a fish leaping out of the sea in agony. Go took pity on them and decided to take the slip off. As he did so, Chigiri's wet body let off an unbelievably strong odor. Go groaned as he held her and her smell. They both stopped thinking of any kind, and moved as naturally as they breathed. Go bit Chigiri's right ear, licked it with his tongue, and blew air into it. The air gradually turned into words.

"When we're like this, I know: 'I love you' are words to say when you face someone. We no longer face each other. We're too close for that. We're layered onto each other. This right ear of yours, it's my ear, and your right breast is my right chest. What this right eye sees is what my eye sees... What did she say the name of the flower in the tokonoma was?"

Trying to calm down, Chigiri looked in the direction Go's eyes were facing, but the flower was enveloped in a hot smoke, and refused to stop swaying back and forth.

"I think it was a cornelian cherry."

"Cornelian cherry? I can see it, too."

A train sounded, far off. You couldn't see it from the inn, but remembering that the innkeeper had said the tracks ran along the coast, Go fell silent.

"What's that sound?" Chigiri asked.

"The train. They run late, don't they?"

"It sounds so close..."

"Then this ear's awfully sharp."

"I had an ear infection once, as a girl."

"Like it's your ear... This is my ear."

And so it went. For a while they earnestly continued an irrational sort of conversation that only the two of them could comprehend. Afraid that silence would sink him deeper and deeper into sadness, refusing to stop at her eyes, ears and breasts, Go's fingers raced up and down the right side of Chigiri's body, turning individual parts into his own.

"The right shoulder won't have it easy. I always swaggered, cutting the air with it."

"The mah-jongg bump on the middle finger."

"That and the writer's bump. It'll be able to identify a tile by touch, and slip *right in* whenever it likes." Go inserted Chigiri's middle finger into her genitals and moved it. For a second, Chigiri couldn't tell whose finger it was. She could feel the yellow petals of the small cornelian cherry falling. Go said, "This finger is better than 'I love you,' don't you think? Now I've become half of you."

Chigiri didn't know whether to laugh or cry. Her face contorted. She thought about how her lips wanted to cry, but Go's lips were smiling. And then something strange happened. She lost the feeling in the right half of her body. It felt as if something or someone other than herself had control over it.

"That's odd! Have you really become half of me?"

Chigiri was serious. It might have been the first sign of an illness that possessed her after she turned fifty. But then again, the heaving emotions of love and the sensitivity of sexual pleasure closely resemble illness.

From that point, Chigiri's physical sensation headed directly into pleasure. It was as if a dam had broken. Her pleasure was Go's pleasure. Her unbridled passion became both of their passion. The shape of the ear was slightly askew, but Go penetrated deep inside of Chigiri, and he ran the gamut from slow to urgent in his movements.

"I can feel it," he said over and over. Half of the burning Chigiri was him, he thought. Go cried out, saying it was the first time he had ever felt this way. Although not words he was used to using, he wasn't embarrassed by them. It was the truth. Chigiri's pleasure far exceeded Go's expectations which meant, of course, that as half of her body, his own pleasure exceeded anything he had hoped for. In instances like this, a man's pleasure might be measurable only in terms of the ecstasy of his woman.

Go was thoroughly satisfied and completely exhausted. Despite the numerous orgasms he sent Chigiri flying into, he was unable to achieve one of his own. The lower half of his body remained excited and full of pent-up frigid heat, but his mind whispered that this was as it should be. He would take the heat with him into the next world. It was a wonderful souvenir of their final time together.

Go slowly pulled out his penis. Chigiri was the one in a stupor. Go continued to caress the cheek, lips, arms and shoulders that were too weak to move. In the process, his nerves were sharpened and polished until they were as sharp and as shiny and clear as a newly-made dagger.

This is the end, thought Go. This is the beginning of something I'll never get through, thought Chigiri, half-asleep.

The next day, Go took a train back to Tokyo from Anamizu Station. The train ride would be easier on him than the drive back to Kanazawa, and neither of them wanted to say good-bye in the middle of a busy city, but it didn't work the way they thought it would. By saying good-bye in a place where there was no one to see their agony, they ended up spilling the tears they had vowed to hide from each other.

When the train pulled in, there would be people on it. Their time alone was over. They had hoped the train would be late—a minute or even a few seconds would suffice—but when they sat down on a bench to wait, it became more than they could bear, and they began to wish the train would come in even a minute or a few seconds early.

They had said and given everything they had to say and give to each other. Go had planned to tell Chigiri that he'd be back to see her because he was worried about her making it safely home. When the time came, though, he didn't want to lie.

"I might go to Tsurugi," he finally said. Chigiri knew he was trying to console her, and did not reply, but gripped his hand tighter. She couldn't bring herself to tell him to "stay well."

She finally managed to say, "Get home safely." And as she did, she felt the right half of her body go numb, just as it had the night before.

"That's my line," Go said. "When you see a red light, be sure to stop. You're the type that will keep on going once you start." They smiled bashfully at each other, remembering the night before.

The train arrived right on time, and their hands pulled apart. Go stood up to leave, and turned around. Chigiri couldn't stand.

"Thank you," he said.

Chigiri responded in kind in the strongest voice she could muster.

It was the fourth month of 1983, two years and two months since their reunion. Go was forty-nine and Chigiri forty-four that spring when *shi* and *ku*, "four" and "nine," homophonous with "death agony," strangely recurred.

And that was the last Chigiri ever heard from Go. Two weeks after they parted at Anamizu Station, Chigiri called his office in Akasaka, but got a recording of an operator saying the number was no longer in use. One day, to suppress an impulse to start calling Tokyo hospitals and track him down, she left the house early and walked around town. Over the next few weeks, every time the phone rang she had to tell herself not to get her hopes up that it might be Go, and indeed, it never was, and still she was painfully disappointed.

About that time, the right half of her body began to experience a nagging pain. It hurt especially at night before she fell asleep. She tried pain relievers and sticking plasters, but the only thing that worked was when she gently rubbed the spot with her left hand.

Mayu was concerned that her mother might be getting arthritis or leading up to a stroke, and pleaded with her to quit her job, but Chigiri continued working at Manraku because she noticed the pain less when she was busy there.

In the fall of that year, on an evening with a beautiful sunset, Mayu came home from school and noticed a black car parked in the road. She walked in, saying since there was a taxi out front, she thought they had company.

"A taxi?" Chigiri asked anxiously.

"No. A black car. It looked like a hired car."

Chigiri ran out in front, and the car quickly pulled away. She thought she saw a man in the back seat. He was hunched down, and she saw a part of his head. Chigiri ran into the street and watched it leave. At the corner where it turned left, she thought she saw the man turn around. The sun in the west was so bright and red, that the sky reflected off the car's rear window was the same color as the red maples of the house next door.

It was February of the next year before she knew for sure who the man in the car had been. On a cold day, she received a package from Hisahiko Ishida in Togi. It contained a dagger, and a note written by Hisahiko that read, "I was asked to send this to you, Chigiri."

Suddenly dizzy, she sat down. It was the dagger Go had promised to return to her.

Are you going to die?

That's what I've been told.

When?

I don't know yet, but I'll let you know when it happens.

How?

I'll send you a message only you can understand.

The message was the dagger. Now she knew Go was gone. She took the dagger in one hand, grabbed her car keys, and ran for the garage. She had replayed that conversation over and over in her mind during the months since it took place. When they had sat on the thick branch of the Rokuro Cedar with Go enveloping her in his arms and the light falling down on them, he had promised that when he died, he'd come back to that spot. He had told her to go there so they could sit just like this together again.

The Rokuro Cedar stood in the middle of the snow-covered fields. There was no wind. The branches and leaves were quiet, and not even a bird sang.

Chigiri marched through the deep snow until she reached the thick branch. She swung a leg over and straddled it just as they had that last time. She closed her eyes and gripped the dagger with both hands. Then she bowed her head, as if it were all part of a ceremony. It was her idea of a woman's funeral.

She slowly opened her eyes to see the one straight branch in front of her. A piece of the bark had been peeled off, and there was something scratched into it. She looked more closely to see that it was a mark about an inch and a half in length that had been carved with a knife. There was a large G enveloping a C; their special ear-shaped mark. It had blackened, and she could see that it had been wet with snow. It had to have been carved before the first snow fell, it couldn't have been later than the preceding fall. It was then that Chigiri understood who had been in the black car.

She began to shiver and placed her lips on the mark. Then her ear and her cheek. This was when she felt something in the right side of her body crack in two.

It was a while later that the owner of the house diagonally in front of the Rokuro Cedar came home and found his driveway blocked by a small car. He called out, "Excuse me, ma'am!" in a loud voice. Chigiri heard him and came back to herself with a start. Still aware of how she must appear to others, she quickly hid the dagger in her sweater.

12

THE 1980S ENDED BUT there were still a few years before the new century. Mayu was just a year away from turning thirty. She had been unsettled and out of sorts. Every time her son, who was now three, began to cry she wanted to cry with him. Instead she was cold and began to take out her frustration on him.

Mayu had graduated from junior college and got a job at a local bank. She met and married a man five years her senior who worked in the lending department. She quit her job when she got pregnant. Her son was healthy, and she was better off financially than most of her friends, but she continued to be plagued by the feeling that something was missing. She wondered if she would take this feeling with her into her thirties.

Mayu's husband was a diligent banker, and she had nothing to complain about, but she had no recollection of ever falling madly, or even moderately, in love with him. She had made the decision to marry with her head rather than her heart, and now her youth was drawing to a close leaving her vaguely unsatisfied.

Another reason for her depression was her mother. Chigiri was ill, and every time they met, Mayu was faced with the problem of what to do about her, and it left her confused—which irritated her more than anything else.

Six years ago, Mayu had married and moved with her husband to an apartment in the Tsukihashi neighborhood of Tsurugi. Her mother had still been in good health, but her husband, out of respect for the strong bond between mother and daughter, had agreed to live there, and commute an hour each way to his bank in Kanazawa.

Contrary to Mayu's concern for her mother, Chigiri seemed content to let her daughter lead her own life, indicating little desire for frequent visits.

Some years before, when Mayu was a teenager and Chigiri was in her mid-forties, she had gone through a long period of depression. At the time she still worked at Manraku, and when she was there, managed to be cheerful, but as soon as she got home, she would rarely speak, and her eyes seemed to focus on nothing in particular. At other times she complained of pain in the right side of her body, and would spend hours in her room. Mayu would check on her occasionally, and see her lying on her bed, curled up in a ball with her eyes closed.

Chigiri had tried to explain away her symptoms as signs of menopause, but Mayu found it all irritating, and the two had frequent arguments.

When Chigiri was forty-eight, Matsuko, a relative who had been the caretaker for an old estate near Heisenji, suffered a stroke and died two days later. Chigiri and Mayu, as her closest relatives, went to take care of her things, but they were at odds the entire time. Matsuko had worked at the estate as a servant, so there was nothing to keep them there after the funeral was over and all of Matsuko's belongings had been sorted out and packed into boxes. But Chigiri stood on the porch and refused to move. When Mayu urged her to leave so they could get back home, Chigiri gave her a withering look. It startled Mayu and gave her the impression she was dealing with someone she didn't really know.

Mayu was anxious to leave this house with its smell of death, and when she told her mother she didn't want to stay any longer, Chigiri turned a deathly pale face on her daughter and told her she was free to go home alone. Mayu was at a loss to understand this behavior. Her only guess was that the deaths in the family were breaking her mother down, little by little. They seemed to make her more angry than sad.

Chigiri spent hours in a preoccupied state, walking up to the second floor of the old mansion and then down to the garden again. Two years later, failing to find someone to look after it, the owners decided to tear it down.

By the time she turned fifty, Chigiri's dark spells began to recede, and, from Mayu's point of view, her behavior became eccentric. One summer day, hearing the engine of the car start, Mayu went outside in her pajamas, only to see her mother driving off in tears.

Chigiri must have seen Mayu come outside, or maybe her reddened eyes had not been able to see anything. She was gripping the steering wheel as if she didn't have a second to lose.

Mayu didn't begin to know where to look, so she sat at home and waited. She finally got a call from Mr. Tokiyama at Manraku. A neighbor had called to tell him that someone who resembled Chigiri was sitting on a branch of the Rokuro Cedar mumbling to herself. Tokiyama asked Mayu to go get her. Since Chigiri had the car, Mayu called her fiancé and asked him to check the Rokuro Cedar to see if her mother was there. His apartment in Tsukihashi, the one they eventually lived in together, was close to the tree. Still in his pajamas, he had gone out looking.

Mayu's fiancé found someone quite different from the Chigiri he had met countless times before. He could never be sure, but he was almost certain that he had seen a young, long-haired girl, with a child-like smile. He suggested to Mayu that her mother see a doctor. It was difficult to say more to a woman he was about to marry, but Mayu understood what he meant. Still she became angry with him. Her mother might be a little neurotic, but she certainly wasn't ill, she insisted.

When they got her back home, Chigiri had a perfectly good explanation for her behavior. She was sorry for worrying them. She'd had trouble sleeping and wanted to go out and hear the voice of the wind. Hadn't she managed to drive to the Rokuro Cedar safely?

When Mayu demanded to know why she had chosen that particular spot, she said that when she sat on the sturdy branches, she could feel the sap gushing through them, and it gave her the energy to keep on going. Her voice was relaxed and her smile uncharacteristically cheerful.

Mayu's fiancé listened in silence, but later insisted to Mayu that anyone else who saw Chigiri sitting there would have known she was ill. When Chigiri said she could feel the sap gushing through the branches, he wondered for a few moments if he hadn't been too worried about someone capable of such a literary sort of remark, but then he thought of the unladylike position in which he had found her. Dressed in a skirt, she had straddled one large branch, and had her ear pressed against a taller one, and was swaying slowly back and forth in a trance-like state. It was definitely strange, but he didn't give Mayu any further description because, until he had intruded on her, the way Chigiri had moved her hips and the way her calm gaze swam across the air in front of her had been sensual in a way that would unsettle a young man of a certain upbringing. His only recourse was to tell Mayu that her mother, the woman about to become his mother-in-law, didn't seem well.

Mayu had accused him of declaring his mother mentally ill and he had apologized. Unfortunately, he had been right, his distance from Chigiri providing the objectivity required in such a situation.

After they were married and Mayu knew she was pregnant, the two went to visit Chigiri in Chimori, and by this time even Mayu had to admit her mother was ill. Chigiri had gone into the kitchen to fix some tea. When she failed to reappear, Mayu went in to check on her and found her curled up in front of the telephone. One hand held the receiver and the other was dialing a number. Each time, however, she hung up before anyone could answer. She repeated the action over and over, unaware of her daughter standing behind her.

"Where are you calling?" Mayu asked,

"Heaven," was the only response Chigiri gave as she continued to repeat the process of dialing and hanging up. Mayu watched her dial, and noticed that the number was different each time. Sometimes she dialed three numbers, sometimes five.

Mayu dissolved into tears. Her husband rushed in to see what was going on. Chigiri put down the phone and turned to look at him, explaining in the most natural way that she was calling heaven to let them know Mayu was pregnant. Mayu was sure she had been the butt of some ridiculous joke, but in the next instant, Chigiri turned to her son-in-law and graciously asked what sort of work he did for a living.

They took her to the Kanazawa University Hospital and she was diagnosed with obsolete epidural hematoma, and was showing symptoms of Alzheimer's disease.

It was an illness that could strike even younger people with symptoms of dementia. The cause was not certain, but she also had temporal lobe disorder, something was wrong with half of her brain. If the hematoma appeared to be growing, surgery would have been called for, but they couldn't get her permission to do it, and her illness was not so far advanced that they could do it contrary to her wishes. Before Mayu and her husband could make up their minds, Chigiri's symptoms began to disappear, and she returned to normal.

"You can't operate on my brain because I might lose my memory. I'd rather die." This was the reply Chigiri gave her daughter, a clear indication of her will, and it was the last time Mayu brought up the subject.

Mayu began reading up on Alzheimer's, and discovered that as long as a patient maintained her general decorum and followed her usual lifestyle patterns and did things in their usual way, even if there were occasional hallucinations and odd behavior, she could generally get along. If nothing happened to frighten her, she would most likely not become aggressive. Mayu decided to let Chigiri continue living alone and keep a close eye on her.

Chigiri's illness would worsen temporarily and then improve, but it was progressing. In the last six months, she had begun to forget more and more words, such as "refrigerator," and "knife," and she had begun getting names and faces confused, too. Chigiri herself appeared aware of her deterioration, and she generally stopped speaking to anyone but Mayu and her family.

One day she looked in the mirror, fluffed up her hair and told Mayu she was very happy. When Mayu saw her mother looking at her reflection and smiling like a young girl slowly losing touch with reality, she locked herself in the bathroom and cried.

After she'd shed her tears, Mayu had to admit to herself that signs of anguish had disappeared from her mother's expression. When she realized her mother was quickly taking up residence in another dimension, she decided she couldn't spend her time sobbing in the bathroom. There was something important the two of them needed to discuss.

Her errand that day was to get her mother's permission to tear down this old house and build a house all four of them could live in together. Her husband, a banker, had already begun to work on the loan applications. Mayu had brought up the subject with her mother numerous times, but each time Chigiri had managed to put on an authoritative expression and insist that the house was fine as it was. But Chigiri was now fifty-nine, and Mayu was determined to celebrate her sixtieth birthday in a new home.

Mayu's son had been playing in the yard with a stray cat, and now came running in crying that he had been scratched.

"Oh, you poor little boy. Go wash your hands and I'll put some medicine on it." Chigiri had pulled herself away from the mirror to look at her grandson's hand. As he ran off, Chigiri turned to Mayu and said, "He's cute. Do you know whose child he is?"

The boy came back and obediently held out his right hand. Chigiri pulled out her first aid kit and, as she rubbed some cream on the scratch on the back of his hand, she spoke to him in a serious tone.

"This hand and the other one belong to different people. When this hand hurts, someone else is in pain, too, so you must be very careful."

The boy had stopped crying, but unable to understand what his grandmother was saying, he was silent. Mayu, of course, had no idea what she meant, but she didn't question her as this sort of statement had become more and more common.

"Mom, we need to talk about this house." Chigiri continued to look at her grandson's hand, turning it over to inspect it. She showed no reaction to Mayu's words, continuing along her own line of thought.

"This hand is heaven's. And this leg, too." The boy pulled the leg under him when Chigiri reached down to touch it.

"Mom, about this house..."

"And this eye..." Mayu grabbed Chigiri's hand that was extended towards her son's face. She pulled her mother towards her, and called her name. The sunshine of the May sky was behind Chigiri, and it was as broad and blue as the sea.

"You're hurting me. I'm trying to tell this child something important. I want him to know that half of his body belongs to someone in heaven."

"Who in heaven? Stop teaching him this nonsense!" As soon as she spoke, Mayu regretted it.

Chigiri stood up and stepped barefoot into the garden, it was as if she was swimming into the light. She stepped through the weeds and sat down formally, her legs tucked under her, in a pool of sunlight. Mayu knew when this happened that there was no getting through to her for a while.

She went back to the kitchen, fixed some fish, boiled spinach, and cooked the rice. Chigiri was able to cook for herself as long as she had familiar ingredients in the house, but lately Mayu had been coming by daily to do the cooking.

She gave her son a cup of juice, and went out into the yard to try and coax her mother back in. Chigiri was still in the same position on the same spot on the weeds, swaying gently back and forth. She was saying something as she swayed. Mayu shushed her son who had come over to talk, juice still in his hand, and crept up behind her mother.

Chigiri was gently rubbing her ear lobe, and whispering in a shaky but seductive voice.

"This right ear of yours, it's my ear… Your right breast is my right chest…"

Oreno… Mayu realized that her mother was using the male form for "my." She stood stock still filled with an unnameable combination of disgust, pity, and envy. Mayu didn't know what delusions were seizing her mother but felt that the deteriorating body enclosed a vast happiness unrelated to her that she would most likely never experience.

The End

About the Author

After working as an editor, Nobuko Takagi won the Akutagawa Prize in 1984 and became a professional writer in her thirties. In addition to the Tanizaki Award for *Translucent Tree*, she has been the recipient of the Women's Literature Award and the Minister of Culture Award. *Translucent Tree* is her first novel to appear in English. The author lives in Fukuoka, Japan.